"LET ME ASK YOU SOMETHING, NICK," CLAY SAID. "WHAT IF BOTH YOUR eyes were bot technology? And let's say you lost your arm, and they gave you a lase arm to replace it? Would you be a person or a bot?"

"A person," Nick said. "I'd be a person."

Clay tapped Nick on his chest again with her finger. "And what if you had a heart attack, and they cut you open and put a fancy bot ticker in there? What then?"

"Then, I don't know, I mean . . ."

"How much of you can they replace and leave you human, Nick Winston?"

BOOKS BY GREGG ROSENBLUM

CITY 1

A **REVOLUTION 19** NOVEL

GREGG ROSENBLUM

HARPER TEEN
An Imprint of HarperCollinsPublishers

To Wendy and Cadence, and the Zoo:
Crash, Furball, and Mia

HarperTeen is an imprint of HarperCollins Publishers.

City 1

Copyright © 2015 by Alloy Entertainment and Howard Gordon and James Wong

Produced by Alloy Entertainment
1700 Broadway, New York, NY 10019
www.alloyentertainment.com

Library of Congress Control Number: 2014942790

ISBN 978-0-06-212602-3

Typography by Liz Dresner

15 16 17 18 19   CG/RRDH   10 9 8 7 6 5 4 3 2 1

First paperback edition, 2016

CHAPTER 1

THEY SLIPPED THROUGH THE ISLAND, CLAY LEADING THE WAY. KEVIN was pushed along by Grennel's impossibly strong grip on his shoulder. Black smoke from the fire curled into the cloudless sky. Another plume billowed up from the south, thickening and covering the southern sky. Was the Wall itself in flames? Not that it mattered—with the control unit stolen from Dr. Winston's lab and tucked away in Grennel's pack, the once-invisible Wall was now nothing more than a pile of burned logs.

Islanders were running toward the southern fire, and in the distance Kevin could hear yells and screams. Not everyone was worrying about the fire, though—they passed near a group of ten Island men who stood in a tight circle, punching and kicking and stomping something on the ground. Kevin caught a glimpse of white neo-plas—a flash of a bot leg—before Grennel hustled him past.

Hiking southwest from the Island, through forest and occasionally along short stretches of a cracked two-lane roadway, Captain Clay pushed a brutal pace all day and into the night. The speed was bad enough, but Clay had also decided to use Kevin as a mule for her gear. He was weighed down with her heavy backpack that felt like it was loaded with rocks.

Kevin stared at Clay's back as he struggled to keep up, replaying those final moments in the laboratory over and over—his grandfather crumpled on the ground, smoke rising from his smoldering shirt; Captain Clay shrugging, then casually telling Grennel to kill Kevin, too, as if she were telling Grennel to step on a spider.

It had been Dr. Winston's dying words—that Kevin was his grandson—that kept Clay from killing Kevin. But Kevin didn't think his reprieve would last if he slowed her down. So he struggled on, hunched forward under the heavy weight of the pack, nearly jogging to keep up with Clay.

Her long arms and legs, lean but muscular, flexed and relaxed, flexed and relaxed—it seemed like she was barely able to keep herself from breaking into a run as she strode along, full of energy that bordered on mania. Her black ponytail, tied with a ragged brown string, bounced with her rapid stride.

"Where are we going?" Kevin said.

Clay ignored him.

When Clay finally stopped walking it was well after midnight. Kevin was so exhausted and dazed that he almost walked right into Clay's back as she stopped in a meadow off the road.

"We'll rest here until daybreak," Clay said, nodding at Grennel, who unshouldered his pack and pulled out two thin bedrolls. They auto-inflated into six-inch-thick mattresses. Kevin didn't bother to ask about a bedroll for himself—he knew better.

He let his pack drop heavily to the ground with a thud. He sat down on the grass, shrugging his shoulders and arching his back, trying to work out the kinks and pinched muscles caused by the heavy equipment. Grennel tossed something into Kevin's lap, and he was so tired he barely flinched. It was an energy paste pack. He had eaten one for lunch, which seemed like a lifetime ago.

"Eat before you sleep," said Grennel. "And drink. We'll be walking hard at first light."

Kevin ripped open the pack and sucked in a mouthful. He quickly washed it down with a swig from his canteen. He hated the bitterness of the paste, and the chalky texture that coated his mouth and made the bitter taste linger. Still, he forced himself to finish it all, grimacing. Grennel was right—if he was going to keep moving, he needed the food.

To Kevin's surprise, both Clay and Grennel lay down on their mats and shut their eyes. Grennel's pack—with the Wall unit inside—rested on the ground near his right arm. Were they really going to leave him unguarded? Kevin almost felt more angry than happy. Did they think he was so harmless, so weak, that they could just go to sleep without him running away? Or—he knew he'd never do this, but still—he could kill them in their sleep, couldn't he?

Kevin lay down, resting his head on his hands. He narrowed his eyes to slits and watched Clay and Grennel. He'd wait awhile for them to fall into a deeper sleep, and then he'd take his grandfather's Wall control unit, and he'd slip away. Clay had no right to it. *She murdered for it*, Kevin thought bitterly. It would serve her right to wake up and find both Kevin and the control unit gone.

He waited, and he thought about his brother and sister, wondering where they were and what they were doing. How in the world was he going to find them? He pushed the thought down. First order of business: Take the Wall unit and get far away from Grennel and Clay. Survive. Find a Freepost. Then somehow get back to his brother and sister.

After twenty minutes, with both Clay and Grennel breathing steadily, Kevin pushed himself to his feet. Moving swiftly, trying to be as silent as possible, he shifted toward Grennel. Twice he froze, holding his breath, as Grennel let out a heavy snore. He finally got close enough to Grennel's pack, and he reached down, slowly, very slowly, to take it.

Grennel's hand shot out like a snake and grabbed his wrist,

and Grennel's other hand clamped over his mouth, stifling Kevin's yelp.

"Quiet," said Grennel softly in his ear. "If the Captain wakes up, it won't go well for you."

Kevin struggled, but Grennel was so strong that Kevin could barely move. Grennel tightened his grip on Kevin's arm, squeezing so hard that it was sure to leave a bruise. Kevin knew that this was just a fraction of Grennel's strength—he'd seen what the man was capable of when they escaped the Island.

Up close, Grennel's sheer size was unbelievable. He towered over Kevin like a tree, and he was twice as broad. His nose was flattened and crooked, obviously broken more than once. He had a long, raised scar that ran jaggedly up his right forearm. Kevin ceased his useless efforts to free himself.

"I sleep lightly," said Grennel. "You won't be able to leave without my noticing."

Still, Kevin considered making a break for it. Would Grennel be able to keep up? Without a doubt, Kevin realized.

"Even if you do somehow manage to escape, it'll be easy enough to track you," Grennel continued. "And then, when you're found, the Captain won't be lenient."

"Then let me leave," Kevin mumbled against Grennel's palm, his breath hot in his own mouth.

The large man shook his head. "I'm sorry," he said. "Really, I am." With a look at Clay, Grennel released him. He bent down and opened the backpack that Kevin had been forced to carry. He pulled out some food packs, clothing, and two small vidscreens. "I can, however, lighten your load," he said. "Tomorrow it'll be less of a struggle for you to keep up."

"Yeah, thanks," Kevin said sarcastically.

"You are welcome," Grennel replied solemnly, and Kevin couldn't decide if Grennel had missed Kevin's sarcasm or purposely ignored it. Grennel carried the gear over to his own pack, and quietly stowed it away. He stood, and pointed at the ground by Kevin's feet. "Sleep," he said. "We've got another long day tomorrow."

Kevin didn't move. Grennel shrugged. "Then stand all night. But don't try to leave again. And stay away from my pack."

Grennel lay back down. Kevin continued to hold his ground, his arms crossed stubbornly. But as Grennel ignored him it didn't take long for Kevin to feel foolish. He cursed, and arranged himself back on the cold, hard earth. Giving Grennel one last glare, it seemed the man was asleep again. How had he moved so fast, and so silently?

Kevin felt like a coward as he lay there with no restraints, no guard. For now, though, he'd have to remain with Clay and Grennel. Find out where they were heading. Figure out what Clay was planning to do with the control unit.

Eventually he'd escape, he told himself. With the control unit. He'd find his brother and sister, and they'd somehow get their parents out of the City, and move to a new Freepost so he'd never have to see Clay or Grennel again. Kevin was cold and scared, and he had no idea how he was going to make any of that happen. It took a long time to finally drift into a shallow, fitful sleep.

It seemed like just minutes later that Clay was roughly nudging him awake with her foot.

Kevin was exhausted after his restless night, but the lighter pack did help, and he was able to keep pace. By midday, however, his legs were aching and the pack felt like it had doubled in weight. He stumbled as he climbed through a dry creek bed, falling to one knee. Grennel grabbed his pack and lifted him effortlessly to his feet. Clay glared back at them, but turned away and kept walking without a word. "We're close," Grennel whispered, too quietly for Clay to hear. "You'll be able to rest when we arrive at the camp." Kevin shrugged out from Grennel's grip, saying nothing, but secretly grateful for the news.

An hour later, a man in dark green camouflage stepped out from behind a tree, a burst rifle slung over his shoulder but pointing at the ground.

"General?" the man said.

Clay nodded.

The man grinned. "It's an honor to meet you," he said. "Follow me, please."

General? Kevin wondered. *Is this some sort of military camp? And Clay's now a general? What happened to "Captain"?*

The man in camouflage led them northwest for ten minutes, following the creek bed, until Kevin could see the campsite—a dozen tents set between trees, a cookfire in a small clearing, a handful of men and women in mismatched military and hunting gear.

Clay straightened her spine and threw her head back, suddenly energized. It was like someone had thrown a bucket of ice water down her back. She strode into the camp. "Greetings, soldiers!" she called out. "It's a joy to finally meet! Are you ready to kill some City bots?"

The rebels gave her a ragged cheer.

Kevin was so bone tired he dropped the pack to the ground and thought about just lying down right there. He wearily looked around the camp, noting the thirty or so men and women, who looked as if they had been living in the woods for a long time—they were all dirty, and thin, and grim. Most had burst rifles slung over their backs, or pistols holstered at their waists.

Then his breath caught in his throat and he choked back a sob. His brother, sister, and Lexi were grinning at him from across the clearing.

They are alive! He hadn't realized until that moment just how hopeless and alone he felt. . . . He took two quick running steps toward them, then halted, his grin dying on his face.

He couldn't let Clay know about them. Better they stayed away from her and didn't attract her dangerous attention.

But of course they were racing up to greet him. Kevin shook his head no, like he could possibly explain everything with just a shake of his head—the Island, the Wall, that their grandfather was Dr. Miles Winston . . . who had been murdered by Clay and Grennel. But Cass reached him first, slamming into him with a hug that almost knocked him down.

"I remember you," she said, squeezing him tightly. "You're back. And I *remember* you."

"You remember me?" Kevin was confused. "It hasn't been that long, has it?"

Cass stepped back, her smile weakening. "For a while, well, I just . . . it's complicated. . . ."

Nick and Lexi reached them. "Kevin! Where have you been? What happened?" Nick asked, grabbing Kevin.

Kevin returned the hug, but saw Clay approaching in his peripheral vision, shaking hands and clapping backs on the way. He stepped back from Nick. "Don't tell her who you are," he whispered urgently.

Nick frowned, and began to say, "What . . ." but then shut his mouth when Clay stepped next to Kevin and laid a hand on his shoulder.

"Seems like a nice reunion," she said to Kevin. "Who are these three?"

"Nobody," said Kevin. He stepped out from under her hand with a grimace. "Just . . . they're people I knew from my old Freepost."

Clay stared at Nick, Cass, and Lexi for a long moment, then looked back at Kevin. "The boy looks like you," she said. "I have more important things to do right now, but that's not something I'll be forgetting soon, Kevin." She strode away, back toward the middle of the camp.

"Rust," said Kevin. "Rust, rust, rust."

"What is going on?" said Nick. "Who was that?"

"She shouldn't know that we're related," whispered Kevin. "It's not safe for you. She's dangerous."

"Who is she?" repeated Nick.

And then Clay began to speak from the center of the crowd, standing atop a small rock. Her voice boomed out. "Fellow rebels!" She paused for effect. "I've been looking forward to this day for a long time. Now that we've destroyed the Island, and its bot lovers, it's time to take back our world. With our courage and our strength, victory is within our grasp!" The rebels cheered.

"I have the tool that we need," Clay continued. "The technology, pried from the hands of a coward, which will allow us to strike directly at the bot-held Cities. We will begin small, but we will be smart and our strength will grow. We will not stop until mankind is free!"

Things began to fall into place for Kevin. That "coward" was his grandfather, Dr. Winston. And the "tool" was the Wall unit she had stolen. *But how will she use it?* he wondered. *To build her own wall? That makes no sense....*

The rebels let out another cheer, and Clay stood quietly, grinning, soaking it in. She raised her hands, and the group fell quiet. She turned and looked toward Kevin. "Nothing will stand in our way," she said. "No bot, no True Believer traitors, no old cowards. We will do what must be done."

Kevin felt a twinge of nervous nausea. "Doing what must be done" had already included destroying the Island and shooting an old man in the back. What would be next?

CHAPTER 2

CASS WAS ELATED TO SEE KEVIN. IT WAS SO STRANGE AND WONDERFUL. She had gotten many of her memories back, but still, they didn't always feel quite true. . . . It was as if some of her recovered memories were just vids that she had watched, lacking sensation, like she hadn't *really* tasted and touched and smelled her own life. When Kevin walked into the camp, though, Cass had felt a twist in her chest and tears well up. This was her brother. This was real, right in front of her, in the flesh. Her memories, her life . . . they were *real*.

It was a relief to have something to be happy about, to distract her, while she waited for the medic, Sarah. Cass was still trying to swallow the news—there was no choice but to amputate Farryn's leg. His pain had become her pain. He had saved her life, protecting her from the bot explosion, and now he might die because of it. The guilt and worry was crushing.

Cass felt her throat drying up with fear as she listened to General Clay speak. The woman seemed to be almost glowing with energy. She was gesturing broadly with her hands, her face locked in an intense grin as she spoke. Her eyes were open wide, too wide, and it didn't seem like she blinked at all.

As Clay explained that nothing, and nobody, would get in her way, Cass thought of her birth parents and her little sister, Penny, back in City 73. They were True Believers, and this woman saw them as the enemy. As no better than the bots. It was crazy to think that Clay and this little band of rebels could do any real damage against the bots, but if they actually could . . . it was clear that Clay wouldn't hesitate to hurt her family and the other humans who "got in her way." Even Nick still refused to understand Cass's connection to her birth family. He couldn't accept that they were really her family, and not just a bot lie. . . .

Giving Nick a look, Cass was relieved to see that he was frowning, his hands crossed over his chest. She had to remind herself that just because Nick didn't understand her birth family didn't mean he was against her. It was complicated, but he was her brother, and he was on her side. She let her breath out, feeling a knot of tension slip away.

General Clay began walking among the rebels, shaking hands, with Grennel sticking close to her side. Cass thought it seemed like a good chance to find out more from Kevin about what in the world was going on, why he was so afraid. It was clear that something was deeply troubling him. . . . It was like he was trying do a million calculations in his head, but kept getting the wrong answer.

"What is it?" she whispered to Kevin, as the rebels began to disperse. "What's wrong?"

But Kevin shook his head. "No," he whispered back. "Not now. I told you, she can't know who you are."

Cass would have found it funny and ironic, if she hadn't been so concerned and confused. The bots had taken away her memories of Kevin, and she had been through so much to regain those memories of him. But now Kevin himself was telling her to pretend she didn't know him. She searched his face for more clues, hoping for eye contact. But he refused to look at her. *Yes*, she remembered. *He can be stubborn.*

Cass saw Sarah the medic striding quickly toward them, and she froze. "Come," Sarah said to Cass. "You still think you can help? I'm ready for the amputation."

Cass felt a swirl of brutal panic at that word—*amputation*—but forced it down. Farryn needed her help. If he died, and she had been too cowardly to help the medic, would she ever be able to forgive herself?

"Cass," began Nick, "I don't think—"

"No," she said, cutting him off. "It's fine. What can I do to help?"

"Amputation?" said Kevin. "Who's getting an amputation?"

Sarah began walking away, with her purposeful stride, and Cass followed, flashing Kevin a quick nervous smile, leaving it to Nick to explain.

"You'll be up at his head," Sarah explained. "No need to watch me working. I don't need you passing out on me."

"I'll be fine," Cass said, trying to sound confident and tough, although she did feel dizzy, and her fingers were tingling. She tucked her long brown hair behind her ears with shaky hands.

"Regardless," said Sarah. "My anesthesia is crude. I'd like you to monitor his vitals for me. Watch his breathing, keep a finger on his carotid. It'll let me focus on getting the amputation done as quickly as possible. If he stops breathing or his heartbeat becomes erratic, let me know and I'll do what I can." Sarah paused outside her tent, and put her hand on Cass's shoulder, looking her in the eyes. "Can you do this? Help me try to keep your boyfriend alive?"

Cass nodded. "I'm fine," she said, forcing herself to sound confident. "And he's not my boyfriend, I mean, not really, I don't think. . . ."

Sarah smiled. "Let's save his life first, and then you can figure that out," she said. She stepped inside the tent. Cass took a deep breath, then followed.

The medic's tent was the largest of all the rebels'—it was pre-Rev gear, not the most high-tech that Cass had seen, but still, it was an auto-construct, auto-breakdown, made of some sort of stiff, treated canvas. The floor was hard, and level, and the ceiling was seven feet high, so Sarah and Cass were able to walk in and stand as if they were in a real room. Lightsticks were hung on each of the four walls and on the ceiling, making the room almost painfully bright.

As if reading her thoughts, Sarah said, "Don't usually waste all these lightsticks. But I need to see when I'm working."

Back near the far wall, on a cot, lay Farryn. His eyes were closed, and he was breathing quickly, almost panting. His hands were folded over his belly. His cheeks were flushed, and his hair was matted down with sweat. He opened his eyes and turned his head to look at the door. "Cass," he said weakly.

Cass froze in surprise—she had assumed that Farryn would already be under the anesthesia—but she quickly caught herself and rushed over to the cot. She took his hand, which was slick with sweat, and squeezed it. He looked at her, his eyes red and unfocused.

"Cass?" he said again.

"Yes," she said. "I'm here."

"My father . . ." Farryn shook his head, as if he was disagreeing with something. "I want . . . and Mom . . ."

"He's weak from the fever and also disoriented from the pre-anesthetic sedative," said Sarah.

"Shh," Cass said. "You're going to be fine." She squatted down on the floor next to Farryn's head, and pushed a slick strand of hair away from his eyes. *He has green eyes*, she thought. *He could be dead soon, this green-eyed boy I hardly know but who seems so important to me.* She fought back the urge to cry. She dropped her hand away from his face and dug her nails into her palm, angry with herself. Crying wouldn't help Farryn right now.

Sarah brought over a small table and a black bag. She began pulling tools and supplies from the bag and placing them on the table. "Don't have any of the right tools for this," she muttered to herself. "Sometimes I think it would be worth it to live in a bot City just to see the inside of a hospital again." She sighed, and picked up an injector. "Still, you've gotta make do. Improvise."

Sarah stepped forward and pressed the injector against Farryn's neck. Cass heard a click and a quiet hiss, and Farryn tensed, arching his back, looking at Cass with panic in his eyes that broke her heart, and then he lay back down, shut his eyes, and was still.

Cass felt an illogical rush of fear—was he dead? Had the medic just killed him?—and then saw that his chest was rising and falling. He was breathing.

Cass reached forward and found the pulse in Farryn's neck.

"The dose should be good for about an hour, but if all goes well I won't need nearly that long to amputate and cauterize."

Cass nodded. She focused on Farryn's heartbeat, slow and steady under her fingers. "Okay, then let's get this job done," Cass said.

Cass made it through the next twenty minutes by focusing on Farryn's heartbeat. She tried, without really succeeding, to ignore the sounds Sarah was making—the whir of a lase saw, the crackling of the cauterizer—and the way Farryn's body was jostled. She thought about all the things the bots had taken away. Her Freepost. Her parents. Her memories. And now, Farryn's leg. The memories could come back. But the rest . . .

"Done," said Sarah finally, with a sigh. She stepped forward and felt Farryn's pulse, gently pushing Cass's hand away. "Thank you," she said to Cass. "Well done. You handled that better than most."

Cass steeled herself, then looked down at Farryn's legs. The right leg, ending just below the knee, was wrapped in gauze. There was blood on the cot and on the floor, but not as much as Cass was expecting.

"So you're done?" Cass said. "He's going to be okay?"

"I'm done," said Sarah. "But now we have to wait and see. I don't have many antibiotics, or painkillers." She wiped her hands on a towel. "Let's hope he survives the next few days."

CHAPTER 3

NICK DIDN'T KNOW WHERE TO GO FIRST. HE WANTED TO STAY WITH Kevin, to find out what had happened to him. He wanted to go with Cass, to see if he could help her and the medic with Farryn's operation. And he wanted to visit Erica, who, unless he could figure out some way to stop it, was going to be executed the next morning.

"Lexi, will you—" Nick began, and Lexi, reading his mind, cut him off.

"I'll go check on Cass," she said, nodding. She touched Kevin's arm. "It's really good to see you," she said, and then hurried away.

Nick put his hand on Kevin's shoulder. "It is," he said. "I didn't know what happened to you. I screwed up. I lost you."

Nick had to pause, to clear his throat and push back the tears that had suddenly threatened to form. "I didn't know if I was going to find you again."

Kevin began to smile, but then he glanced over at Clay, who had just finished her speech and was making her way around the camp greeting the rebels. He stepped back from Nick.

"Not in front of her," Kevin said. "She can't know the truth."

"Who is she?" Nick asked again. It was obvious that Kevin didn't just dislike her—he was afraid of her. "Sounds like she's going to take the fight to the bots. . . . That's good."

"I don't know if anything about her is good," Kevin said. "She's Captain Clay, or General Clay, here, I guess. She was Captain on the Island." Kevin leaned toward Nick, and said in a whisper so low that Nick could barely hear, "She's a killer." He hesitated before continuing. "I met Miles Winston on the Island."

He paused again, and Nick was surprised to see that Kevin's eyes were welling with tears. Kevin looked away, clenching his fists, struggling with something. He turned back to Nick and blurted, "She killed him, Nick! He's our grandfather. Our grandfather! He's dead because of her."

Nick's head exploded with a million questions. Nothing Kevin had just said made sense. He stepped back. "Miles Winston? You found him? And what do you mean he's our grandfather? And . . . this Clay woman killed him? Where were you? What is this Island you both keep mentioning? What happened?"

Kevin looked over Nick's shoulder, his eyes widening for a moment, and then he gave a quick negative shake of his head. "Grennel," he said, shifting away from Nick. "Remember, we're not family."

Nick turned and saw Grennel heading toward them. The man was huge, easily the biggest man Nick had ever seen. This man had killed Miles Winston? And Miles Winston was . . . their grandfather? Nick almost laughed out loud, not because he felt at all amused, but because he was so utterly confused.

Grennel brushed past Nick, giving him a small nod. Nick nodded back, trying to read something from the big man's face. But Grennel seemed calm, almost blank. He certainly didn't seem angry, or violent. Despite his size, he didn't look like a murderer. But then again, neither did the bots.

"Come," Grennel said to Kevin, in a tone that was almost apologetic, but still a command. "The General wants you introduced to the troop leader for assignment."

Nick almost stepped forward—this man had no right to be ordering his brother around, no matter how big he was—but he held back. It wasn't because of Grennel's size, although it was true that Nick would have no chance in a fight with Grennel. It was the quick glance that Kevin gave him that kept his mouth shut. Kevin was saying, *This is important. Stay quiet.*

As Nick watched Grennel lead Kevin away, Nick decided

GREGG ROSENBLUM

that something had changed in his brother in just the short time they had been separated. He seemed a little sadder, a little . . . Nick struggled to pin it down—not more mature, exactly, just *older*. What the hell had happened to his little brother on this "Island"? Nick shook his head, then decided to go find Lexi to see how Farryn was doing.

He made his way across the camp to the medic's tent. Lexi was sitting on the ground outside. "News?" he said.

"Nothing yet," she said.

He glanced at the tent entrance, but hesitated. He knew he shouldn't just barge in during an operation.

"Come on," Lexi said. She patted the ground next to her. "Sit."

So he sat down, tucking his arms over his knees, and waited. Lexi took his hand, and Nick felt himself relax, just a bit. His brother was alive. His sister was getting her memory back. Farryn was in good hands. This new leader—General Clay—something bad had happened between her and Kevin, but at least she would be going after the bots. That would give him the chance to get to his parents.

He was growing impatient. He stood and began pacing. He couldn't stand this waiting, being useless.

The tent flap opened and Cass came out, looking pale and tired. Lexi jumped to her feet. Cass took a deep breath, closed her eyes, and stretched her neck. Nick kept himself from saying anything, waiting for her to speak.

"He made it through the surgery, at least," she said.

"That's good," said Lexi. "That's good, right?"

Cass nodded, without smiling. "The medic says he's not out of danger, though, with the fever and the chance of shock and infection. If he can get through the next few days . . ." Cass paused, hesitated, her cheeks reddening, and then said to Nick, "Was Farryn my . . . I mean, were he and I . . . my memory is still kinda spotty, but it feels like he was . . ."

"No," said Nick, and at the same time, Lexi said, "Yes."

Then Cass did manage a weak smile. "Which one is it?"

"Boys are idiots," said Lexi. "Listen to me."

"That's true," said Cass, her smile broadening a little. "They are."

"Hey, come on now. . . ." said Nick.

Cass sighed, and her smile dropped away. "I'm going to stay with him for a while," she said. She turned toward the tent.

"I'm sure the medic has it under control," said Nick. "Why don't you come rest, or something?"

"No," said Cass. "I want to stay." She disappeared into the tent.

Nick stood there for a moment, feeling useless.

"She'll be all right," Lexi said. "She's tough."

"No doubt about that," Nick agreed. He shrugged. *All right,* he thought. *On to crisis number three.* "Lexi, I've got to . . ." He hesitated for a moment, just long enough to think, *Damn, she's going to know I'm lying,* then continued, "I have to take care of a few errands for Ro."

Lexi crossed her arms over her chest and stared at Nick. "Like I said, boys are idiots," she said. "What are you really up to?"

"I'm going to check on Erica," he said, realizing he couldn't avoid the truth.

Lexi's face darkened. "She doesn't need checking on," she said. "I'm sure her guards have everything under control."

"I didn't mean that," he said. "I meant . . ."

"I know what you meant," Lexi said. "I'm sure they're treating her fine."

"They're going to kill her," Nick said.

Lexi winced, and looked away. "I'm not saying I like that," she said. "But she betrayed us."

"She was trying to protect her family!" Nick said, his voice rising. "I can understand that."

"Oh, really? That's it?" Lexi said, looking back at Nick. "Or is it her pretty eyes?"

"Who's the idiot now?" Nick said. He instantly regretted it, but it was out there.

Lexi opened her mouth to reply, but shut it without saying anything, and spun and walked away.

"Rust," muttered Nick. He watched her go, trying to think of something to say that would make her stop and come back. *I'm sorry* was probably a good start, he knew, but he couldn't make himself say it. He shook his head. "You *are* an idiot," he said to himself.

CHAPTER 4

KEVIN STOOD SILENTLY AS GRENNEL BRIEFED RO ON KEVIN'S SKILLS. He'd been forced to skip dinner and it looked as if he'd be expected to work through the night. It was clear that his training was being put to work as they readied the camp for battle. He'd be assisting the tech officer, a short, thin man named Stebbins, with the warning that if Kevin got lazy he would be put on grunt work for the camp.

As the moon crossed the sky, Kevin spent an hour with Stebbins fixing two broken ear comms, some frayed portable gridlines, and a power supply for a burst rifle that wouldn't recharge. He tried to keep up a pace that was quick enough to keep him away from any manual labor—he didn't want to dig latrines—but not so slow that he looked incompetent.

Kevin soon realized he didn't need to worry. Stebbins was busy taking apart two vidscreens and was ignoring Kevin completely. He rubbed his eyes, fighting sleep.

Kevin was studying the rifle's power supply—he had already repaired it, but had a tenuous idea for boosting its power—when Clay and Grennel returned from a camp meeting.

Stebbins jumped to his feet. "General," he said, offering an awkward salute.

Clay grimaced. "We don't salute, if that's what that was," she said.

"Yes, uh, sorry," said Stebbins.

Clay glanced over at Kevin, who quickly looked down at the rifle power supply, pretending to be tinkering with it. He saw, in his peripheral vision, that she continued to stare at him for a few moments before turning back to Stebbins.

"Grennel," she said. "The Wall unit."

Grennel handed the Wall unit to Stebbins, and Kevin's heart began pounding harder. He listened carefully, and watched as closely as he could without staring.

"As we discussed," she said, "I need this adapted to cloak an individual as quickly as possible."

Stebbins nodded, already absorbed in examining the unit.

"Stebbins," Clay said.

He pulled his attention away from the unit and looked at her.

"End of the day," she said. "You have until the end of the day to show me something good." She took a step closer to him.

"I will not be happy if you fail. And if I'm unhappy, you will be extremely unhappy. Understood?"

Stebbins, suddenly pale, nodded.

Of course, Kevin thought. Clay was trying to cloak a person. It was exactly the kind of use that Clay would want for his grandfather's technology—the ultimate camouflage gear. Perfect for attacking a City.

Stebbins spent the rest of the night and into the next morning examining the Wall unit and weaving conduction wire into a helmet and hunting vest. Kevin spent a few hours sleeping with his head on the table, and the rest of the time spying on him while pretending to be fixing the tech he had already repaired.

From what Kevin could see, it looked like Stebbins was trying to create a limited circuit for the cloaking field. But—*rust*—what would the cloaking field do to a person? Wouldn't it kill them? The Wall at the Island wasn't damaged by the cloaking energy, but a wall wasn't alive. The metal pylons in the Wall probably had served to ground the energy, as well as provide structural support. But how could Stebbins create body armor so the wearer didn't get electrocuted? And also, how would Stebbins make sure the power didn't overload? The control unit was designed for a huge wall, stretching across a mile of perimeter—that much juice would be massive overkill for a single six-foot person.

But Kevin kept his thoughts to himself. It wasn't as if

Stebbins was asking for his help; if Kevin said anything, he'd just end up digging ditches, or worse.

As the sunlight began to fade, Clay and Grennel came, as promised. Clay brushed past Kevin without even looking at him. Grennel nodded as he strode past, but Kevin didn't acknowledge him.

Stebbins jumped to his feet. Clay was a full head taller than him and looked down at him with her hands on her hips. "Status report," she said. "Make me happy."

Stebbins cleared his throat. "Just finished a first proto-type," he said. "I'll need a more elegant way to patch into the control. It's kind of clunky right now, and I still have to fig-ure out how to disperse the field across multiple units without being tethered to the control unit. . . . I'm not sure if that's even possible, really. . . ."

"Does this one work?" interrupted Clay. "Give me one working unit first, and then we'll worry about the other problems."

Stebbins nodded slowly. "Yes, I've tested it very briefly, just for a few seconds. . . . I didn't want to damage the con-trol unit—that probably wouldn't have made you too happy." Stebbins tried to smile and chuckle, but he turned the laugh into a cough when he saw Clay's glare.

"And the cloak worked?" said Clay.

"Well, the vest and helmet disappeared, yes," said Stebbins.

"And the person wearing it?" said Clay.

Stebbins frowned. "Well, it hasn't been tried on a person yet."

Clay said nothing for a moment, then said, her voice tight with controlled anger, "This needs to get done, Stebbins. We can't just sit around and wait for you."

"It's ready," said Stebbins, hoping to placate Clay. "I'm sure of it."

"Let's see, then," said Clay.

"Yeah, uh, yes, of course," said Stebbins.

"Now," said Clay.

Stebbins carefully slipped on the vest and set the helmet over his head. Kevin, dropping all pretense of working, took a step toward him for a better look. He could see, now that he was able to directly study Stebbins's worktable, that he had created a lattice within the vest that clipped to the helmet for a complete circuit. And the gear was patched directly to the control unit with a thick conduction cable that ran like an animal's tail to the rear of the vest. *The energy field should definitely generate*, Kevin thought—the person would be invisible. But what was he using to modulate the power? Kevin couldn't see any external control or power soak. He felt a sudden queasy burst of unease. Could Stebbins really be so dumb that he was going to run the full power of the unit through this tiny circuit? With himself inside it?

"Step back, please, for your safety," said Stebbins. He had a line of sweat running down his cheek. He looked like he'd rather be just about anywhere else. Clay and Grennel moved back.

Kevin looked over Stebbins's work again. It was true—there really didn't seem to be any kind of damper on the power. He knew he should say something—it could be dangerous—but he kept quiet. This was his grandfather's technology, technology that had been stolen from him. That he had been murdered for. Why in the world should Kevin help Clay?

So Kevin said nothing as Stebbins took a breath, then flipped the switch on the control unit, which was attached to his vest by a short wire. There was a hum that set Kevin's teeth on edge, and Stebbins disappeared. Clay yipped and clapped her hands. Then, echoing her shout was a loud crackling *pop* and burst of light that momentarily blinded Kevin. He flung his arm over his eyes reflexively, and when he lowered his arm, blinking painfully, he saw Stebbins's convulsing body. "Turn it off!" he yelled.

Grennel rushed forward and switched off the unit. Stebbins stopped flopping, and lay motionless. Grennel reached down and felt on his neck for his pulse. "Dead," he said, standing up slowly.

Clay rushed forward to the control unit and began examining it. "If that idiot damaged the unit . . ." she said. She set it back down after a few moments. "It's okay, I think," she said, with relief.

Kevin stared down at Stebbins. The acrid smell of burned

hair and skin reached him. For some reason, he had still thought Stebbins would be safe. People don't die for reasons like this—if only Kevin had opened his mouth and stopped Stebbins, the man would still be alive. But instead . . .

Clay whirled to face Kevin. Kevin tore his eyes away from the body of Stebbins to meet Clay's stare. He forced himself not to flinch.

"What did you do?" Clay said quietly.

"What are you talking about?" Kevin said, confused.

"Did you sabotage Stebbins?"

"No!" said Kevin. "He didn't modulate the power. The idiot didn't even try to modulate the power."

Clay stared at him. "And you said nothing," she said. She hesitated, then smiled that vicious, unsettling smile of hers and tapped Kevin on the chest with her finger. "You've just got a promotion," she said. "Head of tech development. You're going to build a new suit, and you're going to test it on yourself, so I hope you do a better job than that fool over there." She gestured down at Stebbins.

Kevin realized he had been played, and he cursed himself for being so blind. It had all been a test to trap Kevin into creating the ultimate betrayal to his grandfather. The breeze shifted and the smell of Stebbins's body hit him again—the sulfurous burned hair, the charred flesh—and he had to swallow hard and clench his fists to keep himself from throwing up.

CHAPTER 5

ERICA'S EXECUTION HAD BEEN DELAYED WITH THE ARRIVAL OF CLAY, but still, any day now, she'd be dead. Unless Nick could figure out some way to help her.

Nick leaned against a tree while he watched Erica twenty yards away. She sat on the ground, legs crossed, forearms on her knees, staring unfocused at the distance, a shock collar glinting on her neck. Four metal posts formed a small square perimeter around her, and one guard, a man everyone called Rabbit, stood outside the perimeter. Rabbit was small, but Nick had seen him fight—both against bots and in a camp fistfight after a card game—the man was lightning quick. Probably why they called him Rabbit.

Rabbit looked bored, leaning against his burst rifle that

was propped on the ground. He didn't have much to do. . . . If Erica stepped outside the perimeter her collar would trigger and she'd be unconscious, if not dead, within seconds.

Erica turned her head, saw Nick, and gave him a thin smile and a nod. Nick nodded back, resisting the impulse to wave—that would have been dumb . . . to wave at a girl who was waiting to be executed. Instead, he took a deep breath and walked toward her. She stood, brushing the dirt off her pants.

Rabbit perked up from his glazed boredom when he saw Nick approaching. "No visitors, Nick," he said.

"You okay?" said Nick to Erica, ignoring Rabbit. "They treating you all right?"

Erica nodded. "Good enough," she said. She didn't say anything else, but she continued to stare at Nick.

Damn, Lexi, thought Nick, *it is true . . . she does have pretty eyes.*

"I said no visitors," said Rabbit, his voice picking up an edge of anger. He stepped between Nick and Erica, rifle in hand.

"Sorry," Nick said, looking down at Rabbit. He wondered if he could take the man in a fight. Rabbit was wearing a comm bracelet—it was probably patched into Erica's shock collar controls. If Nick could get the man down, maybe even knock him out, he could take the bracelet and figure out how to turn off Erica's collar, and Erica would have a chance to escape.

Rabbit apparently saw something in Nick's face that he

didn't like, and he took a small step back and moved his hand closer to the trigger of his rifle.

Nick saw the subtle move. "No problem, Rabbit. I'll go." It had been a stupid thought. Even if he could take Rabbit down so quickly and quietly that nobody else noticed, the comm bracelet was most likely bio-flagged to work only for Rabbit. And if he somehow figured out how to power down Erica's collar, what then? When Rabbit woke up, Nick would find himself the one inside a shock perimeter, with a collar around his neck.

"Hang in there, Erica," Nick said.

Erica sat back down and resumed staring off into the distance. "It's all right," she said, without looking at Nick. "I did what I thought I had to, and now Ro is doing what he thinks he has to."

Nick said nothing. Erica had been working for the bots, it was true. Because of her, rebels were dead . . . and Nick could have been dead, and Cass, and Farryn. He should have felt nothing but anger. He should be looking forward to her execution. But instead, he understood. He truly did. She was doing everything she could for her family. It was wrong, it was selfish, but it made sense. He came to a decision.

"And I'll do what I have to do," he said.

Rabbit tensed, and put his hand on the trigger of his rifle. "Don't," he said. But that wasn't what Nick had in mind. He turned away without another word and walked off.

Nick found Ro at the southern edge of the camp. With General Clay. The two were looking at a vidscreen Ro held, discussing something quietly. Nick hesitated, then continued forward. *Might as well take it all the way to the top*, he thought. He had only taken a few more steps forward, however, when a strong hand clamped down on his collarbone and spun him around. Nick found himself looking up, way up, at Grennel. Nick could see that the big man had a thin, pale scar that ran along his right cheek, just above the line of his beard.

"Where are you going, son?" said Grennel.

Nick tried to shrug out from under Grennel's hand, but Grennel just tightened his grip and held Nick in place.

"I need to see Ro," Nick said, gritting his teeth against the pain.

"He's meeting with the General," said Grennel. "I don't think she'd appreciate the interruption."

"I should see her, too," Nick said. He tried again to pull away from Grennel but almost went down to his knees from pain as the man dug his fingers around Nick's collarbone. "Let me go," he hissed.

"Happy to," said Grennel. "If you're planning on turning around and walking away."

"Ro!" Nick yelled. "We need to talk!"

Ro looked up, frowning, and Grennel gave another twist into Nick's skin. Nick gasped and this time he did find himself on his knees, trying to pry Grennel's vicelike grip off him before his collarbone snapped. He could feel his muscle grinding against the bone. . . . Something was going to give.

"Grennel! Let him go!" It was Clay who spoke.

Grennel immediately released Nick, who took a moment to get to his feet. His right arm hung numb and useless. Nick tried to rub feeling back into his shoulder and arm.

"You'll be fine in a few minutes. Just pinched the nerves a bit," said Grennel.

"Come!" said Clay, gesturing at Nick.

Nick, still rubbing his dead arm, glared at Grennel, then turned and walked to Clay and Ro.

"What the hell are you doing, Nick?" said Ro.

"It's all right," said Clay, holding up her hand. "I've been meaning to speak with you." Ro crossed his arms over his chest, obviously angry, but he kept quiet.

Nick began to feel electric tingles in his arm, which was good—the feeling was coming back. He stopped rubbing his shoulder, and, meeting Clay's stare, suddenly wondered what he had gotten himself into. General Clay, up close, was just as intimidating as from a distance. It wasn't her physical presence, though, although she was tall and leanly muscular. She was even, in a certain harsh sense, attractive. It was her eyes that made Nick afraid. They were, in their own way, just as strong as Grennel's grip. She expected respect; you could see it in her gaze. Obedience. Discipline. And she looked utterly, wildly confident . . . like someone who had never had a moment of self-doubt in her entire life.

"I want . . ." Nick hesitated, then reminded himself, *This is the right thing to do*, and pressed on. "I want you to reconsider Erica's execution."

"She's a traitor, Nick," said Ro. "It doesn't matter what history you may have with her—"

"Enough," said Clay. Ro cut himself off in midsentence. Clay walked toward Nick, stopping just a few feet from him. She smiled, and Nick flinched briefly before catching himself. "Why should I spare this girl, Nick? She was passing intelligence to the bots. She is a traitor." Clay spit the word out like it was a curse.

"They have her brother," Nick said. "The bots were going to kill him. She was just trying to protect him."

Clay scowled. "At what cost? She keeps her brother alive as a slave to the bots, and in return, she betrays all humanity."

"It's not that simple," said Nick. "She's not a bad person. She saved my life. . . ."

"No, it is simple, Nick," Clay said. "Everything in this screwed-up mess of a world is simple. It all boils down to one question: bots or humanity. She chose bots."

Nick was silent, at a loss. There was nothing he could possibly say to change this woman's mind.

"Nick," said Clay, "you have a family?"

It took a moment for Nick, confused by the subject change, to respond. "Yes," he said.

"A brother?" Clay said quietly.

Nick hesitated. *Rust*, he thought. This was going badly. . . . Kevin had been adamant that Clay not know about Nick and Cass.

Clay didn't wait for Nick to answer. "Kevin is your brother, correct?"

"No," said Nick. "Kevin, he's just someone I knew from my old Freepost. Not my brother."

"Yes," said Clay, nodding. "Interesting. More Winston brats."

"Really, he's just an old neighbor," said Nick, sounding false even to his own ears.

"Enough," said Clay, with an edge in her voice. "You're starting to insult me." Clay turned to Ro. "This traitor, Erica. We are scheduled to execute her tomorrow?"

"Yes," said Ro.

"Good," said Clay.

"Wait!" said Nick, struck with a desperate idea. He turned to Ro. "We still have her comm device, the one we took out of her leg?"

Ro nodded.

"Put it back in her," Nick said.

"I don't understand," said Ro. Clay raised her eyebrow, but remained silent.

"Keep her alive. Let her plant false intel with the bots. She can be useful."

Clay smiled coldly. "Okay, Nick Winston. I'll keep your

traitor friend alive, for now. We'll see how useful she can be. But"— she paused, cracking her knuckles—"her behavior, and her usefulness, is on your head. You'll be guarding her. If she damages our cause again, I will kill her. And I will probably kill you, too."

"You're welcome to try," Nick said. It was stupid, and Nick knew it—but after all he had been through, he was not going to be bullied. Not by bots, not by humans. He could feel his cheeks burning and waited tensely for Clay's reaction, shifting his weight to the balls of his feet, clenching his fists, ready to fight or run.

Instead Clay just laughed. "Wonderful!" she said. "I like your spirit." She poked him in the chest with a finger, hard enough to make Nick flinch. "Your brother is the smart one, and you're the brave one."

Clay came closer to Nick's face as something new caught her attention. She looked directly into Nick's eye. "Nice piece of hardware you have in your face, there," she said. "How'd you get it?"

"The bots," Nick said.

"Care to elaborate?" Clay said.

Nick knew he couldn't lie, but he wasn't about to tell Clay his life story. "My Freepost was destroyed, and I spent some time in a City before I escaped. The bots fixed my blind eye."

"Very generous of them," Clay said. "I've been briefed by Ro. Apparently you're quite the marksman. Because of the eye?"

Nick just shrugged.

"Let me ask you something, Nick," Clay said. "What if both your eyes were bot technology? And let's say you lost your arm, and they gave you a lase arm to replace it? Would you be a person, or a bot?"

Nick said nothing.

"I asked you a question," Clay said.

"A person," Nick said. "I'd be a person."

"And what about your legs?" Clay said. "What if they blew off your legs when they attacked your Freepost, and they gave you some nice new bot legs to walk around on?" Clay tapped him on his chest again. "And what if you had a heart attack when you watched your home being destroyed, and they cut you open and put a fancy bot ticker in there? What then?"

"Then, I don't know, I mean . . ."

"How much of you can they take away and replace, and still leave you human, Nick Winston?"

"It's just an eye," Nick whispered.

"Yes, right," Clay said. "Well, I'll be keeping my eyes on you. Both of my human eyes."

CHAPTER 6

CASS STAYED WITH FARRYN ALL DAY AFTER THE AMPUTATION—SARAH HAD other duties to attend to, and could only check in on him occasionally. She taught Cass how to take his vitals, keeping track of his heart rate and fever, and how to inject saline if he wouldn't drink, to keep him hydrated. But ultimately, Sarah warned Cass, there was little they could do at this point. "The fight," she said, "is his to fight. You should go and get some rest." But how could Cass leave him? He had lost his leg for her. He might die for her. The least she could do was watch over him while he struggled.

Farryn thrashed and groaned, flushed and sweaty with fever and pain. Cass held his hand, which was slick with sweat, and tried to remember all of the times they had spent together. What had still slipped through the cracks of her mind?

Sarah came back into the tent and checked on them both. She bent down, resting on her knees, and quietly watched Farryn for a few moments. Cass found it unnerving, the way she just looked at Farryn, as if she were deciding something.

"What is it?" Cass said, trying to keep the anxiety out of her voice. "Is he okay?"

"Any spike in the fever while I was gone?" Sarah asked.

Cass shook her head. "No."

Sarah stood up slowly, grimacing and rubbing her left leg. "Damned knee," she muttered. "No change," she said. "Fever's creeping up a bit, but not spiking too badly. The cauterization is holding clean, no suppuration, although it would be too early for that, really."

"So why . . . it looks like you think something's wrong."

Sarah shook her head. "I'm going to give him another dose of synth-morphine, and an antipyretic to keep the fever in check, but that's going to be it for the painkillers. I can't spare any more." She sighed. "When this dose wears off in about four hours, I know how much he's going to be hurting."

Sarah prepared an injector, and pressed it against Farryn's neck. Farryn tensed, then relaxed with a sigh. He opened his eyes and looked up at Cass, his bloodshot gaze focused for the first time in hours. He reached out his hand to her and she squeezed it gently. He actually managed a weak smile, which seemed to Cass like the bravest thing she had ever seen. "It'll be okay," he whispered.

"Yes," she said, a tightness in her throat. "You're going to be fine." *How could* he *be trying to comfort* her?

He closed his eyes, his breathing slow and steady, and she held his hand as he drifted into sleep. She thought, unexpectedly, of the self-portrait she had sketched for him, and how he had kept it, folded carefully away, all this time.

"Go," said Sarah. "He's going to sleep for a while. Get some rest yourself. Go for a walk. Get some food. No need to stay here."

"I'll stay," she said. What if he woke, and he found himself alone? She had to be there when he needed her. When he could look at her and somehow smile.

Cass curled up on the floor next to Farryn and closed her eyes. She thought about how different her life could be right now. She could be with her birth sister, Penny. What was she doing right now? Was she on top of a tower in Hightown, looking out past the rooftops of the bot City, out at the patch of green forest where Cass was? Was she thinking about Cass?

She tried to reach out with her mind, like she used to do as a little girl, back in her Freepost shelter. As she fell asleep, she would reach out with her thoughts to the forest, trying to find the minds of the rabbits and the squirrels and the deer. Of course it didn't work then, and it didn't work now. Cass drifted into a fitful nap.

She woke, disoriented, to Farryn's moaning. She jumped to her feet. How long had she been out? How could she have fallen asleep? Sarah was in the tent, bending over two injectors. She pressed one against each side of Farryn's neck. Cass was expecting to see Farryn relax, but the medicine didn't seem to have any effect—he continued to groan and shift back and forth in the cot, his eyes shut, hair matted with sweat, cheeks flushed.

"Why didn't it help?" Cass said.

Sarah didn't look up from watching Farryn. "It was just antipyretic for the fever, and saline. Can't do a proper drip out here in the damned forest. I warned you I can't do much for the pain now. I just have to hope I can keep him hydrated and keep the fever down enough until it breaks on its own."

"What if the fever doesn't break?" said Cass.

Sarah shrugged casually, but her voice was sad, and angry. "Then it means he's dealing with a systemic infection, and losing the fight." She held her hands out, palms up. "I've got no antibiotics to give him. It's like the damned nineteenth century out here. He's lucky I'm not bleeding him with leeches."

"But he won't die," said Cass, a statement more than a question.

"He's young." Sarah shrugged. "He has that in his favor."

Cass pushed back the panic. *He will pull through.* She walked up to the cot and stared down at Farryn. She could feel the heat rising off him. She asked herself, yet again, why she cared so much about this boy. Her memories of her time in the City with Farryn were still not entirely back—there were a few blank spots—but she knew that he had risked his life for her, and her brothers, more than once. And that he had a way of grinning at her that was somehow simultaneously teasing and earnest. And that he had kept her artwork. That he had done the most to push her back to being herself.

A shaft of light flashed inside the tent, illuminating Farryn's pale face. Cass turned and saw the big man—Grennel, the general's bodyguard, or assistant, or whatever he was. He stood in the entrance to the tent, holding the flap open, leaning forward awkwardly to fit his huge bulk into the small enclosure. He nodded at Cass. "Come with me," he said. "General Clay wants to see you."

"He might die," Cass said, her voice barely more than a whisper. "Farryn could die, and I won't be here."

"He's in good hands," said Grennel gently. "We have no choice here. You must come."

CHAPTER 7

KEVIN WORKED THROUGH THE NIGHT, BREAKING FOR ONLY A FEW HOURS to sleep and eat before returning to work. But it was one step forward and two steps back with the camouflage project.

He thought he had found a way to tamp down the power with an improvised ground, a fairly simple soak that ran about two-thirds of the Wall unit's power to a broken circuit and diffused the extra energy. It worked—at least the body armor was rendered invisible, and hopefully the field would be strong enough to cloak the wearer's entire body from head to toe.

But there were a few flaws. First, the leeching power emitted a buzz that was loud enough to hurt Kevin's ears from twenty feet away, and it wouldn't do much good to be invisible if you were buzzing like a giant hive of bees. Second, the broken circuit, a conduction wire trailing down the back of the suit, sparked and sizzled and even set a patch of grass on fire. Again, not ideal to start a fire and burn your calves when trying to sneak into a City.

Still, on the bright side, the temperature inside the suit rose only marginally in the fifteen seconds that Kevin had let the system run before having to shut it down to save his hearing and prevent a forest fire. Which meant that the suit could—theoretically—cloak a person and not kill him.

Kevin couldn't help thinking about Stebbins as he worked. The man should still be alive. Kevin could have opened his mouth; he had known the wiring was dangerous. But he had said nothing, and Stebbins had died a horrible death. Nobody blamed Kevin; in fact nobody in camp seemed to care much about the death of Stebbins at all. But Kevin knew.

In the short time that Kevin had known Stebbins, he hadn't seemed like a bad man—he had just been stuck working for Clay. He probably was unaware of the Island, and the blood on Clay's hands.

Kevin, on the other hand, knew all about Clay, about what she had done to get the control unit. And yet, here he was, tinkering away at his murdered grandfather's tech, working for the murderer. He had thought about refusing, and letting Clay or Grennel do whatever they would do, but it wasn't that simple. It was so complicated, in fact, that it almost made Kevin dizzy thinking about it.

Clay was smart; he knew that she had already figured out that he had a connection to Nick and Cass. If Kevin refused to work, he didn't doubt that Clay would be willing to hurt his brother and sister. And, as much as he hated Clay, he had to admit that the idea of attacking the Cities with the cloaking tech, of bringing the fight to the bots instead of just running and hiding, was appealing. How else would they have any chance of rescuing his parents?

Kevin struggled for another hour. He tried coiling the loop, which he thought might disperse the heat, but actually did nothing. Then in a burst of misguided inspiration, he built a makeshift flared tail out of cabling, hoping that spreading the grounding wires might do the trick. It fanned out like a claw. Anyone wearing the unit would look like a peacock—not the best way to be stealthy, but Kevin just wanted to see if would help. He tested it, and within a few seconds there was a painful glare, then a pop, and the claw-tail began to smoke and crackle. He quickly turned off the power and threw down his tools. He closed his eyes, resting his head on his palms. He was so tired and stressed—all he wanted to do was sleep and then wake up and find himself back in his Freepost, with his parents and his brother and sister and Tech Tom, working on a grid repair, tending the flock, even taking a forestry hike. . . .

"I'm guessing that's not what you were intending," said Nick. "The smoke and fire, I mean."

Kevin started, jumping to his feet. He hadn't heard Nick coming. "Actually it is," he said. "Firestarter. For campfires. Just working out a few details."

Nick nodded, smiling, but his smile dropped away quickly. "Seriously, Kevin, what's going on?"

Kevin didn't say anything. He looked around, to see if anyone was nearby. They were alone.

"Kevin, come on," Nick said quietly, leaning in. "You've got to talk to me. You found Miles Winston? General Clay killed him? What the hell happened to you? And Stebbins—word is he died in an accident. What happened?"

Kevin shook his head, blinking back tears. "Not safe," he said, not trusting himself to say anything more without losing control and crying.

If Nick had gotten mad at him then, which is what Kevin was expecting, then Kevin would have stayed resolute and kept quiet. Instead, Nick nodded and sighed. "All right, Kevin," he said. "Whatever you've gotta do." He turned and began to walk out of the workshop.

"Wait," said Kevin. And slowly at first, then his words picking up speed and almost tumbling over one another, Kevin told Nick everything that had happened to him. Being captured in the woods by Winston's bots. Having his nose broken. Being taken to the Island. Working on the Wall. His friends Otter and Cort and Pil. The bot 23. Miles Winston, and how Kevin had discovered that he was their grandfather. And then the treachery of Clay—how in order to steal the Wall technology she had brought about the uprising by having that girl that Otter liked, Wex, killed. How Grennel had shot their grandfather in the back and Clay had left him for dead. That the only reason she hadn't killed him, too, was because she thought it was interesting and possibly useful that he was Winston's grandson.

Last, he told Nick about Stebbins, how he had forgotten to ground the circuit and ended up killing himself. Kevin left out the part about knowing it might happen—he couldn't get himself to admit that out loud.

"And that's why I don't want her knowing about you or Cass," Kevin finished. "You're safer if you just stay away from her. Don't make her interested in you."

Nick sat down heavily, staring over Kevin's shoulder. "It's probably too late for that," Nick said. "She knows we're brothers. I'm not sure what she knows about Cass, but she'll probably figure that out, too."

Kevin nodded. He wasn't surprised—it was silly to think that he could keep Clay away from his brother and sister.

"How do you even know that Miles Winston is our grandfather?" Nick said.

"He had pictures of Dad when he was young," said Kevin. "He knew I had an older brother. He even looked like us. And . . . he even kinda sounded like Dad, the way he said some words."

Nick shook his head in disbelief. "Dad never would talk about his family. Now we know why, I guess. It's because his father basically built the bots."

"Dr. Winston didn't mean for all this to happen," Kevin said, surprising himself with how forcefully he said it. "He felt terrible about it. It was all he could think about."

"But he wasn't doing anything about it," said Nick.

"No," said Kevin. "No, he just wanted to hide in his Island. But I think maybe he was ready to change his mind and fight the bots. Then he was shot."

Nick said quietly, "I should just get us out of here. We're not safe with Clay."

"She'll get us into the City," said Kevin. He couldn't just leave his grandfather's work in Clay's hands. Something good had to come out of all of this. "And with the tech I'm working on, we'll be able to get Mom and Dad out."

Nick shook his head and frowned. "I don't like any of this. I don't want you ending up like Stebbins. Don't do anything stupid."

Kevin didn't want to think anymore about Stebbins, so he forced himself to smile. "You mean stupid like giving myself up to sneak into re-education?"

"Yeah," said Nick, cracking a small smile. "Or attacking a sphere bot with a homemade overload box and your jacket."

"I'll try to avoid that," said Kevin.

"Good," said Nick.

"So," said Kevin. "Farryn . . . what exactly happened to him?"

"A fight with the bots," Nick said. "Farryn protected Cass from an explosion, and the medic had to amputate his leg. You should visit him when you can. He'll want to see you."

Kevin tried to absorb that information, subconsciously touching his own calf. He couldn't picture Farryn with only one leg. How in the world was he going to survive in the woods? Was he going to hobble through the forest on crutches? There was no way Clay was going to wait for him, if he couldn't keep up. If only Farryn could spend a day in a rejuve tank—or just nanosolder on a new one, like a bot. He stared at Nick, suddenly conscious of his bot eye, and then the idea hit him, in that lightning-flash way that solutions often did. He could help Farryn, and figure out the problems with the cloaking tech. . . .

He needed to get back to the Island.

CHAPTER 8

GENERAL CLAY SAT ON THE EDGE OF HER COT, SIPPING FROM A STEAM-
ing tin mug and watching Cass. Neither had spoken. If Clay
wanted to sit here for two hours, then Cass would stand just as
long, and as quietly, and stare just as hard.

Clay set her mug down on the floor next to her cot. "You
don't seem concerned by the situation you are in," she said.

"What situation is that, exactly?" said Cass.

Clay smiled humorlessly, and looking at that thin smile,
Cass started to feel afraid. "You're in my camp. Surrounded by
my guard, in my tent. And I do not like True Believers. I find
them"—she paused, looking for the right word—"abhorrent."

Cass felt herself flushing with anger. "I am not a True
Believer!" she said.

"But you have been through re-education in a City. You have lived among the bots, correct? As a . . . what do they call you traitors? As a 'loyal citizen'?"

Cass bit back another angry reply. Clay was baiting her. She took a deep breath. "The bots had me . . . they had me confused for a little while. But I'm over it." Cass paused, and then, because she couldn't help herself, she added, "You would have been confused, too. Anybody would have."

General Clay surged to her feet, and Cass took a step back, surprised by the sudden movement. Clay stepped closer to her. "I would never have been confused," she said with quiet anger, leaning in toward Cass's face. "The bots are the enemy." Clay stood up straight and flashed that chilling smile again. "It's very simple," she said, calm again. "The bots have enslaved humanity. They are the enemy, and anyone, any human, who sides with them, is also the enemy."

"No, it's not that simple," said Cass, thinking of her birth parents, and her sister. Her sister had been born and raised in the City. . . . She didn't know anything different. Was she a traitor? Was she the enemy?

"Yes, it is," said Clay. "It most certainly is."

Clay sat back down. "Would it interest you to know that I, too, have been in a bot-controlled City?"

Cass said nothing.

"After the Revolution," continued Clay. "Were you even alive during the Revolution?"

"I was a baby," said Cass.

"Well, I was a captain in the North American Air Defenses. And we were useless, all of us . . . so dependent on the bots to fight for us that we could barely even fight for ourselves. We were herded up just like all you civilians. I spent two weeks in what used to be Montreal, in a holding pen, while the bots decided what to do with us. They didn't have re-education back then—most of us military, they decided to kill. Some became traitors and helped the bots, providing logistics and intel, and they were spared. And some of us, like myself and Grennel, escaped."

Clay leaned forward, her hands on her knees. "Tell me, Cass, how did you leave the City? Why were you allowed to leave?"

Cass didn't like where this was going. "I don't know," she said. "I don't really remember . . . I didn't understand. . . ."

"Right," said Clay. "So what I have here is a girl who was re-educated by the bots, then released for some unknown reason and brought to my camp. Are you a spy, Cass?" She waved off Cass's reply. "No, I do believe that you think you have recovered. I don't think you are, consciously at least, a spy. But the bots have not been, in my experience, stupid. Why would they let you go? Perhaps you are a sleeper agent of some sort? Maybe they've created some sort of mental trigger, some sort of timer in your brain?" Clay again flashed that thin, creepy smile. "Maybe I'm being a little too creative."

She stood, opened a trunk next to her cot, and took out her pistol and belt holster. She strapped it on with fluid, unconscious ease, then rested her right hand on the butt of the gun. "Tell me, Cass, just to be safe, wouldn't it be prudent for me to just kill you so I won't have to worry about you?"

Cass felt frozen. Her fingers tingled. "Like the bots did to the military?" she said quietly, almost a whisper.

Clay laughed, a short, bitter, humorless burst. "No, Cass, not like that." She stood quietly over Cass, her hand gripping the butt of her gun. Cass shifted her weight to the balls of her feet and tried not to stare directly at the pistol in its holster. She glanced over her shoulder. Should she try to run? She held her breath, and waited.

Clay stared at her, her hand still on her gun, her forefinger tapping the metal trigger guard. She frowned, and sighed, and moved her hand away from her gun, and Cass let her breath out. "No," Clay said. "I don't think so. You interest me, Cass. I'll let you live. For now. And you're going to work for me."

CHAPTER 9

NICK WOKE, GOT DRESSED, AND WENT TO THE LATRINE TO RELIEVE himself, then headed to the creek to splash cold water on his face and neck. He returned to camp and found Lexi, who was stretching and yawning outside her tent.

"Breakfast?" he said.

Lexi nodded. She seemed to be in a peace-making mood. He was grateful that she had let their fight pass. They made their way to the central fire, where that morning's cook—the rebels rotated the duty every few days—had roasted a spit of squirrels, put two pots of coffee on solar-heating units, and harvested a pile of apples.

Nick had learned that Lexi didn't like to talk for a while in the morning, so he didn't try to make conversation. They ate quietly. At least this way he couldn't say anything stupid, he figured. It was a blessing.

Nick jumped to his feet when he saw the medic approaching him, a black bag slung over her shoulder. His first thought was that Farryn had died, but why would Sarah be going out of her way to tell him? Could something have happened to Cass? To Kevin?

"Ro told me to bring you," said Sarah. "I'm operating on the prisoner, that girl Erica."

Operating? What's happened to her? And then he realized . . . they must be planting her spy chip back in.

Sarah looked back and forth between Nick and Lexi, shooting him a meaningful glare. "If you've got something going on with this girl, I don't care about that one way or another. But don't interfere with me while I'm working. Understand?"

"I don't have anything going on with Erica," Nick said, painfully aware of Lexi's presence next to him.

Sarah shrugged.

"I'm coming, too," Lexi said.

"No, sorry, the General has a specific list," said Sarah. "No party crashers."

"It'll be okay," Nick said, and then, trying awkwardly to lighten the mood, he added, "Save me some squirrel." Lexi didn't smile.

They cut through camp and approached the segregated area where Erica was being held. A small group was waiting—Ro, arms crossed, frowning; Rabbit, scowling at Nick with a burst rifle slung at the ready; and of course Erica, fatigue evident on her face, the shock collar tight on her neck, but standing up tall and defiant.

Ro uncrossed his arms and pointed a finger at Nick. "Not one word," he said slowly. "I have little patience for this. The General wanted you here because she wants to remind you that Erica is your responsibility. But keep your mouth shut." He waited, and Nick kept quiet, although it was a struggle.

Ro nodded grimly. "Good." He turned to Sarah. "Let's get this over with."

Erica said to Ro, "You're just as bad as the bots."

"You don't know what you're talking about," Ro said. "You've betrayed us, and we're still giving you another chance. Would the bots do that?"

"Some chance," said Erica. "You're going to use me to pass bad intel to the bots. How long before they figure it out and kill my brother?"

"It's a chance," repeated Ro. "A better chance than being executed."

"Just a delay," Erica said.

Ro seemed about to say something else, but instead he shook his head in disgust and spoke to Sarah. "The comm chip is ready for reinsertion?"

Sarah shrugged. "As far as I can tell," she said. "You would activate it with a special pattern of pressure on your leg, right?" she asked Erica. Erica nodded, and Sarah continued, "Should hopefully just be a matter of sticking it back in there."

"Good enough," said Ro. "Sarah, begin."

Sarah set down her bag and opened it. She pulled out a white linen cloth, which she lay on the ground, and then set an injector, scalpel, tweezers, and a few other tools Nick didn't recognize on the cloth. "Erica," she said, "pants off, and lie down on your side."

Erica, without hesitation, unbuckled her pants and stepped out of them. She was wearing tight black boxer shorts as underwear. Her thigh, where they had cut out the implant just a few days ago, was still bruised, with a jagged half-healed scar. She looked around the circle defiantly, refusing to be embarrassed, and Nick felt himself blushing.

Sarah made quick work of it, injecting Erica with a local anesthetic, then embedding the comm chip back near the spot from which it had been roughly gouged out. She closed the incision with a small lase-like device that fused the skin together. "Would be nice if I had antibiotic," she said, to no one in particular. "No point in saving her from the hangman if we just let her die from an infection." She helped Erica back to her feet. "Leave the incision site alone for an hour or so. It'll give the chip a chance to resettle itself properly into your muscle. You might unseat it if you start poking on it right away. And try to keep it clean. Like I said, I don't have any antibiotics for you."

"Okay, we're done here," said Ro. "Show's over. Rabbit, get Erica set up with a tent. Keep an eye on her. Either I or the General will be there in an hour. Nick, you'll be relieving Rabbit soon. Keep an ear on your comm." He handed a headset to Nick.

Nick took a step toward Erica, and Rabbit quickly stepped between them. Nick ignored him, looking over the man's shoulder at Erica. "You okay?" he said.

"You're not responsible for me. I don't care what Ro says," she answered, surprising Nick with the venom in her voice. "Whatever I do, whatever happens to you, it won't be my fault."

CHAPTER 10

IT TOOK A MOMENT FOR KEVIN'S EYES TO ADJUST TO THE DIM GLOW OF the lightstick hanging from the ceiling. He saw Farryn lying on a cot at the back of the tent, and Cass sitting on the ground, her back against the bed. She stood and quickly crossed the small space, giving Kevin a hard hug. "His fever finally broke," Cass said. "The medic says that's good, that's really good."

"That's great," said Kevin. He looked at Farryn, who was sleeping with his mouth hanging open. Kevin felt a sick jolt, even though he was expecting it, when he saw Farryn's gauze-wrapped leg ending just below the knee. He pulled his eyes away, and stepped back to look at his sister. She looked tired, and somehow older. Kevin had heard bits and pieces of Cass's story, enough to know that she had been back in the City, and had a rough time of it. *It's no surprise,* he thought, *that she looks worn out.*

Still, that was no reason to stop treating her like his sister. "You look like hell," he said.

Cass raised an eyebrow. "Yeah, thanks. You look crappy, too."

"Well, at least we're both looking better than Nick," Kevin said.

"True," said Cass with a small laugh. She stood back from the cot so Kevin could get a better look at Farryn.

Kevin took a step toward the cot, studying Farryn. His hair was matted down with sweat, but the color of his cheeks looked normal, and his breathing was slow and deep.

"He was shielding me when he lost the leg," said Cass, looking down at Farryn. "It's going to be really hard for him, out here. It would even be hard for one of us, and he's a City boy."

"We'll help him," said Kevin. "I have an idea." He hesitated. How could he say this so it wouldn't sound crazy? Just spit it out, he decided. "A bot leg," he said.

"What are you talking about?" said Cass. Farryn groaned, and shifted in his sleep. Cass continued, whispering, "We're just going to ask some Lecturer bot to donate a leg and then glue it on to Farryn?"

"Neo-plas," said Kevin. He kept his voice quiet, but he grew more excited as he spoke. "Lightweight but tougher than real skin. I can probably salvage some of the basic circuitry, maybe even rebuild it. If this medic is good, maybe we can attach his nerves to some nanocircuit grafting, give him basic functioning. That would be crazy fletch, actually, and even if we can't pull that off, it'll still be a better fake leg than anything else we could get."

"Kevin, slow down," said Cass. "I still have no idea what you're saying."

"I'm saying," said Kevin slowly, for dramatic effect, "that I'll go back to the Island and get one of my grandfather's bot legs. I just need to convince Clay."

"How are you going to do that?"

"Trust me, sis." Kevin stepped out of the tent with a quick smile. His plan had to work—he could kill two birds with one stone, if Clay bought his plan.

Kevin hurried across the camp to Clay's tent. Grennel sat at a table outside, studying something on a small vidscreen that Kevin thought looked like a toy in Grennel's huge hands. He flicked the screen off and stood when he saw Kevin approaching.

"I need to talk to her," said Kevin.

"Kid, you know I can't let you in there," Grennel replied as he stood to his full height.

"Look, Grennel, this is important—" began Kevin, cutting himself off when Clay stepped out of her tent.

"It's fine, Grennel. Stand down," said Clay.

Grennel nodded and stepped aside.

"If I were you," said Clay, "I'd be spending all my time

figuring out how to keep that camouflage vest from frying you instead of bothering me, but it's not my life on the line."

"That's exactly why I'm here. I need to get back to the Island," Kevin said as calmly as possible.

There was a moment of quiet. Grennel raised his eyebrows and turned to look at Clay. Her face was expressionless. "Why, exactly, do you need to go back there?" she said.

"Tools, from my grandfather's workshop," Kevin said. "And neo-plas. And other supplies. I don't have what I need here for the camo suits."

Clay stared at Kevin. "The Island has been attacked by bots. It wouldn't be a safe trip."

Kevin swallowed the angry reply that wanted to come out—*it was attacked because you destroyed the Wall.* "Look," Kevin said, "you can keep me here and I won't be able to fix the camo suits and then you can fry me in one of them and you won't be any closer to having your cloaking tech." He took a breath. "Or, you can let me go scavenge what I need."

Clay was silent for another few seconds, then nodded. "Fine. You can go—escorted, of course. And you *will* hurry back." She cleared her throat. "I know Nick is your brother, and Cass is your sister. I'm not a fool." Clay smiled. "I'll kill them both if I find out that you've been wasting my time."

Kevin ate a hard biscuit and an apple. He sat on the ground, hands on knees, washing down the dry, tasteless biscuit with sips from his canteen, waiting for Grennel as the sun rose on a new day. He was so nervous he could barely eat—if this trip to the Island didn't go well, it would be bad not just for him, but for Nick and Cass, too.

Finally he saw Grennel approaching with a man and a woman he didn't recognize. Kevin stood, his legs stiff from the cold ground. *Might as well get this out of the way.*

"This is Oswald, and Wynn," said Grennel. The man and woman nodded. They were both short and lean, especially standing next to Grennel's hugeness. The man had a way of walking, catlike almost, that hinted at him being very quick and athletic, and the woman had a white scar along the jawline of her left cheek that made her look almost comically tough.

They nodded at Kevin, and he gave them a small nod back. "Grennel," he said, "I've got one important condition for going on this trip."

Grennel folded his arms over his chest. "You're not doing us any favors here. The General, in fact, is the one being generous. You're in no position to be setting conditions."

"Yeah, well, I'm setting one anyway." Kevin hesitated, then plunged forward. "When we get there, you've got to let me bury my grandfather."

Kevin thought—or did he imagine?—that he saw a hint of surprise flicker across Grennel's stoic face. The big man said nothing, just stared at Kevin. Then he unfolded his arms and said, "Yes. I agree. If it's safe, and we have the time. I'll help."

"No," said Kevin. "You won't help. You'll leave him alone." Letting Grennel help with the burial, Kevin felt, would be somehow forgiving him. As if it would be letting Grennel atone for what he did. "Just agree to let me do it."

Grennel closed his eyes, holding them shut a few moments too long to be a blink, then reopened them and nodded. "Okay. I agree. Let's go."

Kevin followed Grennel and the others toward the eastern edge of the camp. He wanted to say good-bye to his brother and sister, but he wasn't sure if Grennel would wait. He also didn't want to make too big a deal out of his going, had tried to keep it a secret. But when they reached the eastern perimeter, Kevin found Nick, Cass, and Lexi waiting near the sentry. Kevin had to suppress a smile.

"Trying to sneak out?" said Nick.

"Damn it," said Kevin. "Thought I could avoid you all. How'd you know I was leaving?"

"Nothing stays a secret for long here," Cass said, wrapping him in a tight hug. Lexi followed with a peck on the cheek. Nick, however, turned to Grennel and said, "I want to go with you."

Grennel shook his head. "No."

"I don't need babysitting," Kevin said, angry.

"I know that," Nick said. "But I can help."

Grennel shook his head again. "Out of the question," he said.

Nick stared at Grennel, and there was a tense silence while everyone waited for Nick to react. Finally he turned to Kevin. "Be careful," he said.

"It's hopefully just a few days," said Kevin. "No big deal."

"We all just found each other," said Nick. "Don't get lost again."

Kevin knew that Nick was expecting a sarcastic or annoyed reply, but instead he said solemnly, "I'll be careful. I'll come back, I promise." He held his hand out.

Nick took a moment to clear his throat—Kevin was surprised to see that Nick seemed to actually be fighting back tears.

CHAPTER 11

CASS WATCHED HER LITTLE BROTHER WALK AWAY, BACK INTO THE WOODS, and her instincts told her that it was wrong, that the bot leg was a crazy idea, that they needed to stick together. But she didn't say anything. He thought he had to go, and she had to let him try.

She gave Nick a quick squeeze and a nod as she left him with Lexi. It was too painful to discuss what would happen if Kevin didn't come back. She wanted at least one untainted memory of them all together, sticking together.

She had some time before she had to check in with Clay, who had given Cass a long list of chores. She crossed the camp, walking silently so as not to disturb the handful of rebels who were still asleep, or attract the attention of the people who had already risen and were going about their morning routines—eating breakfast, shaving, rolling their bedrolls.

She found Sarah sitting on a small folding chair outside the med tent, eating an apple. She nodded at the tent. "Your boyfriend's doing much better. Had a good night's rest. No more sign of the fever."

"He's not—" began Cass.

Sarah held up her hand and interrupted. "Yeah, I know, he's not your boyfriend. Whoever he is, he'll be able to start moving around today, which is good, because I doubt we're going to stay in this camp much longer, and I don't think this general is the type to be taking it slow for men who can't keep up."

"No," said Cass. *No doubt about that*, she added to herself. "Can I go in?"

"Go ahead," said Sarah.

Cass entered the tent and stood near the entrance for a moment, letting her eyes adjust to the low light.

"Hey, Cass," said Farryn, his voice quiet and weak, but clear. "Come in."

Cass was amazed, despite Sarah telling her he was doing better, to see Farryn sitting up on the edge of the cot. He looked tired, but he had healthier color in his cheeks—a more natural pink under the scruffy stubble, no longer the madly flushed cheeks surrounded by paleness when he was fighting the fever.

She looked down, just for an instant, at the stump of his leg, before quickly catching herself. Farryn shifted the bedsheet to cover his legs, and Cass felt a pang of guilt—not just for staring at his leg, but for him being injured in the first place.

"I'm sorry," she said, staying by the entrance of the tent.

"For what?" Farryn said.

"That you got hurt."

"It's not your fault," he said.

"You were protecting me," she said.

"Yeah," he said. "Pretty gallant, you have to admit." He smiled at her, with his almost-mocking but still-sincere grin, and Cass found herself smiling back. She walked over and sat down next to him on the cot.

"Yes," she said. She picked up his hand. "Very impressive."

There was a silence, then, as Farryn looked at Cass, his grin slowly dropping away. Cass thought, *Oh, rust, he's going to kiss me.* Farryn cleared his throat and looked away, and Cass stood up, dropping his hand, relieved, mostly.

"Cass," Farryn said quietly, and Cass realized that he was fighting back tears. He cleared his throat and began again. "Cass, I don't know how I'm going to keep up, with just one leg."

"You'll be fine," said Cass. "We'll help."

"I mean it," said Farryn, meeting Cass's eyes intently. "I'm a cripple. I can't be holding you back. It won't be safe for you."

Cass's reply caught in her throat. Even scared, he was still thinking of her first. She crossed the distance between them, barely thinking about what she was doing, and kissed him hard on the lips, hands on the back of his head. Farryn froze for an instant, then put his arms around her and returned the kiss.

Cass broke away from Farryn. *Did I really just do that?* "Have we . . . uh . . . have we done that before?" she said.

"No," said Farryn. "Not like that."

Cass felt her cheeks burning, and she suddenly had no idea what to do with herself. She coughed, and looked away, crossed her arms, uncrossed them, looked back at Farryn, who was still watching her.

She got angry at herself for being so flustered. *It was a kiss. I kissed him. Congratulations. Now move on.* "No more cripple talk," she said.

"Cass, look, I'm just saying . . . ," he began.

"No," she said, angrily. "I don't want to hear it. There's no time for pity, and you don't need to score any more gallant points with me, okay?" She lowered her voice, and continued, more calmly, "We're not leaving you behind, and you won't be a problem. Kevin . . ." She began to tell him about Kevin's plan, but stopped herself. He really wouldn't want to know that Kevin was trying to harvest a bot leg for him. "We'll figure it out," she finished awkwardly.

Farryn nodded. "I may need the occasional morale boost, though," he said. "That kiss, for example, that was very helpful. . . ."

Cass felt her cheeks start to burn again, and she was having trouble coming up with a good reply, but she was saved by the tent flap opening, letting in a bright slab of natural morning light.

"One last look at you, before I kick you out of my tent," said Sarah, brushing past Cass. She set her black bag against the wall, then stood over Farryn, hands on her hips. "I'll take another look at the wound, then get you on your way. The sooner you get up and moving, the better, now that you're past the worst danger. I'm not running a hotel here." She looked up at Cass, and gestured for her to come closer. "Let me show you how to check for infection, clean the wound, and re-bandage," she said. "You've got the stomach and the head for it, and I'll be needing the help once the fighting starts, I'm sure."

She knelt down and began to move the sheet, but Farryn stopped her. "Hold on," he said. "Cass . . . you don't . . . you should go."

It hurt, to see him suddenly look ashamed. She didn't care about seeing the stump of his leg—the surprise was beginning to wear off. But she understood. "Okay, I'll see you soon," she said.

"Come back when you can," said Sarah. "I'd like to show you a few things."

Cass nodded, and left.

She was still a bit in shock as she walked slowly toward Clay's tent. That had been her first kiss, as far as she could remember, beyond a few ridiculous dares at kidbons that were more jokes than anything else. What had surprised her most was how she had launched into it before she even realized what she was doing. She smiled, thinking about how shocked Farryn had been, how she had almost knocked him over.

And then her smile died as Clay, standing outside her tent, came into view. She was wearing camo pants and a short-sleeved green T-shirt that looked like it was a pre-Rev synthetic. The shirt was sleeveless, showing Clay's lean, strong, tan arms, and Cass could see, as she walked up, a black tattoo on her left bicep. It was an eagle, with a fierce beak, and outstretched talons that were dripping blood.

Clay glanced up from the vidscreen she was holding for just a moment, noting Cass's presence.

"So you saw your brother off?"

Cass didn't reply.

"Suit yourself." Clay turned her attention back to the vid. Suddenly Clay's comm piece buzzed, and a voice came through. "General, we need you on the other side of camp to review the armory." Clay looked annoyed, but reluctantly got up. She stepped into her tent, then reappeared a few moments later without the vid.

"Back in five minutes," she said. "Wait here." Clay strode away, south, quickly disappearing into the trees.

Cass stood there, feeling like a fool. And then she had an idea, and before she could think about it too much, and decide it was insane, she went ahead and ducked into Clay's tent. A quick look at the vid—maybe she could find something useful, some hint about the General's plans. Grennel and Clay were constantly referring to the vidscreen—it had to hold some special type of information . . . and if she knew Clay's plans, she could maybe help her birth parents. Was she really going to attack a City? How could she possibly? What was she planning to do with the True Believers? Her City parents—would Clay have them killed?

Cass looked around the small, tidy tent, her heart pounding. She had to move fast, but she also had to be careful. . . . Clay would know if anything had been moved around. . . . Cass opened a canvas pack that was propped up against the bedroll. Spare socks. A few shirts. A pair of pants. She moved the clothes as little as possible, trying to see if anything was underneath, seeing nothing. She closed the pack, then stood, and looked around again. What else? She should probably get out of the tent. . . . It would be bad, very bad, if Clay caught her in here. It was a stupid, probably pointless risk, she admitted, and she was about to leave the tent, when she found it.

The vidscreen was tucked under the pillow on the bedroll. She lifted the pillow and tapped on the dark screen. It flared to life, glowing brightly, asking in black lettering for a password. "Rust," she whispered. She tapped the screen again, to turn it off, but the screen continued to glow. Feeling a twinge of panic, she searched along the sides of the vid, looking for a switch, a button, but there was nothing. "Idiot," she said. Kevin would know what to do, how to turn the damned screen off. But Kevin wasn't here, and she had to turn it off herself, and she had to get out of the tent. . . .

She tapped on the screen a few more times, accomplishing nothing, the screen still glowing, still asking for a password, and she was starting to hyperventilate because her five minutes had to be almost up. Desperate, she placed the pillow back over the glowing vid and hurried outside. She knew she'd see Clay standing there, probably with a blast rifle already in her hands. . . .

Clay was nowhere to be found. Cass breathed a quick sigh of relief, then felt a sick rush as Clay appeared, coming back up the path. Ten more seconds . . . if Cass had stayed in the tent just ten more seconds, she would have been caught. *Stupid, stupid, stupid*, she thought. She tried to slow her breathing, to calm her thumping heart. She forced a look of what she hoped was calm and boredom onto her face. As long as Clay didn't go back inside for her vid, and as long as the damned thing eventually turned itself off. . . .

Clay nodded at Cass. "Come," she said. "I have work for you." She walked back down the path, away from the tent, away from the glowing vidscreen under her pillow, and Cass, dizzy with relief and still silently berating herself, followed.

CHAPTER 12

THEY HEADED EAST OUT OF CAMP. IT WAS A CHILLY, CLOUDLESS MORN-
ing, and the glints of sunlight through the trees hurt Kevin's
eyes, so he kept his head down. Grennel walked in front, leading the way, and Oswald and Wynn trailed behind Kevin.
Being back out on the trail, separated again from his family,
heading back to the Island . . . Kevin couldn't decide if he was
excited or scared or sad.

Nobody spoke. They just walked, stopping occasionally for
Grennel to check his bearings on the tiny vid built into his
wrist comm. It had grown into a warm day after the damp
morning, and Kevin's back was soaked with sweat under his
pack. At lunchtime they continued their silence, until finally
Kevin couldn't take it anymore. He turned to Oswald and

Wynn. "So what's your story?" he said. "How'd you end up with the rebels?"

Wynn frowned, which made her scar appear bigger. "I tried Freeposts for the first few years after the Revolution, but I preferred fighting to hiding."

Kevin waited for more, but apparently Wynn's speech was over. She went back to her lunch. "What about you?" Kevin said to Oswald.

"None of your damned business," Oswald calmly replied.

All right, then.

Kevin slept poorly that night. He dreamed about his grandfather being lased, and Tech Tom strapped to the cold metal slab, and his mother looking at him with confusion, not knowing who he was. Three or four times he woke, his heart pounding, sitting up to catch his breath and get oriented, and each time he saw a different guard on watch in the murky starlight. First it was Grennel, then Wynn, and finally Oswald. Grennel and Wynn ignored him, but when Kevin woke during Oswald's shift, the man turned to look at him, swinging the muzzle of his burst rifle toward Kevin. Oswald held his gun pointed toward Kevin, who lay back down and waited, watching the whites of the man's eyes glowing in the moonlight. *The sclera*, he could hear his mother's voice telling him. *The whites of the eyes are called the sclera.*

Kevin woke in the early morning light, more tired than when he had gone to bed. He stood, and yawned, and bent down to roll up his pack, and then he heard the crackle of underbrush from the far end of the clearing, twenty feet away. Oswald yelled, "Cover!" and swung his rifle from his shoulder into his hands, and Kevin felt a blur of motion as Grennel rushed past him, toward Oswald. Oswald triggered a crackling burst just as Grennel flew into him with his shoulder, knocking him sideways.

There was a scream, and at the edge of the clearing a man fell to his knees, clutching his right arm.

"Idiot!" said Grennel, looking down at Oswald, his foot on Oswald's rifle, pinning it to the ground. This was the first time, Kevin realized, that he had seen Grennel truly angry. "You shoot before you even see what you're shooting at?" He kicked the rifle away from Oswald's hand, then hurried over to the man who had been shot. Kevin and Wynn followed close behind.

The man was pale, his face dirty, with a patchy, thin beard, and he was obviously in a great deal of pain. He held his arm tightly against his body. His shirt arm was burned ragged, and Kevin could see, under the man's hand, the blackened skin of the lase wound on the man's bicep.

"Who are you?" said Grennel.

"You shot me," the man said between teeth clenched in pain. "You didn't have to shoot me."

"You're right, we probably didn't," said Grennel. "Who are you?"

"I know you," said the man. "You're Grennel. From the Island. I'm from the Island, too." He rocked back against his ankles, and closed his eyes. "Ah, rust, this hurts!"

Grennel reached down and helped the man to his feet. He kept his hand on the man's good arm. "What are you doing out here?" he said.

"I'm just . . . I don't know. I got out, after the bots attacked. I didn't know if anyone else got away. . . ."

"Bots?" said Kevin. "You mean the Governor's bots? Like 23?"

Grennel glared at Kevin, but didn't say anything.

"No," said the man. "No, we ripped apart all the Island bots. . . . I'm talking about after . . . after the fighting. The real bots came. The City bots. They bombed the Island, and they killed us, and they took us away. They took the Governor away. . . ."

Grennel tightened his grip on the man's arm. "The Governor? The bots took the Governor?"

The man nodded. "I saw them taking him out of his lab. I was hiding under a section of the Wall. . . . They blew up the Wall. . . . They had lased him."

No, thought Kevin, *it wasn't the bots that lased him.* Grennel gave Kevin another look, a warning, and Kevin kept quiet.

"Oswald!" Grennel called.

Oswald walked up. "He came bursting into our camp," he said. "It looked like he had a weapon."

"Shut up," said Grennel. "Patch him up, and take him back to the General's camp."

"But my orders were to help guard the boy—" began Oswald.

Grennel stepped toward Oswald. "Deliver him safely or you'll answer to me. Understood?"

Oswald nodded. "Got it," he said.

Grennel looked back at the injured man. "My apologies," he said. "Oswald will take you to safety. He won't shoot you again."

The dazed man could barely grunt in reply.

"This is worse than our scouts expected," Grennel said to Kevin and Wynn. "Let's go see what's left of the Island."

Kevin could smell the Island before he saw it. There was a smoky char in the breeze, like the ashes of a campfire.

And then he saw the remains.

The Wall, completely exposed without the control unit, was in ruins. The wood logs lay twisted and cracked and burned in toppled piles. Here and there, throughout the timber, the veins of conduction wire glinted in the sunlight. Sections of the Wall still stood, refusing to topple completely, leaning at awkward angles.

Kevin was remembering Freepost chaos—screams, neighbors lying broken in the dirt, smoke, and explosions. He hadn't let himself think about his devastated Freepost, his home, his friends, in weeks. But he couldn't hold back the memories as he stood there, staring at the wrecked Island Wall and the burned and crumbled buildings beyond.

Grennel nudged his shoulder, hard enough for him to stagger forward a step, making him trip over rubble.

"Come," said Grennel. "Let's not linger. In and out." He began walking between the two piles of wrecked lumber and conduction wire that used to be the entry gates.

"You did this," Kevin said to Grennel's back as he followed the huge man.

Kevin thought he saw Grennel's shoulders stiffen momentarily, but the movement was so quick he might have imagined it. "No," Grennel said without looking back, or even slowing his stride. "The bots did this."

"They couldn't have done it without your help," Kevin said.

This time Grennel did stop and turn. "I don't help the bots," he said slowly. His face and voice seemed calm, but there was a hint of anger just beneath the surface. "I fight them. I do what has to be done to help the General, because she'll do whatever it takes to defeat the bots."

"Including this," Kevin said, nodding at the destruction they were about to enter.

Grennel held Kevin's stare for a moment, then turned away and walked into the wreckage. Kevin followed.

Fifty feet into the Island, Kevin saw the first corpse. He noticed the man's arm first, sticking out from under a pile of stone from a collapsed wall. The skin was pale and the fingers were clenched into a claw shape. Then he saw the rest of the man, partially covered under the rubble, easy to miss if you weren't looking right at him. He was dead, unquestionably dead, eyes open and staring up unblinking into the sun.

"Rust," Kevin whispered. How many more were there going to be? Was he going to find Otter, or Cort, or Pil, lying in the dirt?

Grennel glanced back at Kevin, then followed Kevin's gaze to the corpse. "Come on," he said, his voice, Kevin thought, surprisingly gentle. "Keep moving. We have one hour."

At the mess hall, they found three more bodies. These were badly burned, and their limbs were twisted at odd angles—it looked as if they had been hit by an explosive. Kevin couldn't even tell if they had been men or women. He clenched his jaw and looked away, fighting down a wave of nausea and fear.

"We should—we should bury them," he said. They couldn't just be left like garbage on the ground.

Grennel shook his head. "No time," he said.

"So we just leave them here?" Kevin asked angrily.

"I'm sorry," Grennel said. "It would take too long."

Kevin shook his head, frustrated, although he had to admit, a small part of him was relieved that he wouldn't have to handle the corpses. He forced himself to look away from the bodies, to push the horror and disgust back. He had a feeling he'd be having nightmares about those bodies, sometime soon . . . but for now, he had to focus. He searched the ground, moving rubble with his legs and hands. He had seen 23 and a few others of his grandfather's bots taken down here by the angry mob—hopefully they were still here, somewhere. . . .

He searched for a few minutes, Grennel and Wynn joining in the search, although he didn't tell them what he was looking for. And then he saw it: fishbelly-white neo-plas skin, under a plank of wood. He pulled and pushed the wood out of the way, unearthing one of the Island bots. *Was this 23?* Kevin wondered sickly, as he stared down at the bot. He couldn't tell—the bot's face had been crushed, the neo-plas and leather patches shredded and ripped, and there was no way for Kevin to know if the pattern of leather patchwork had been 23's. He studied the body, surprised that he felt almost the same level of unease as he had when staring at the human corpses. He clenched his jaw. *Enough*, he told himself. *No time to be a baby.*

He examined the bot's body more closely. It was missing its left arm, and its chest cavity had been scorched, like it had been hit by a lase. Both legs were intact. *Good,* he thought. He'd figure out how to detach one, or just hack it off somehow if he had to, although he did want to preserve the circuitry and mechanics as much as possible . . . and then he realized something, so stupid it almost made him laugh out loud. He wasn't sure which of Farryn's legs had been amputated. He tried to picture Farryn, in the cot, one leg unnaturally short, wrapped in gauze—he thought it was the right leg, but he wasn't sure.

He shook his head ruefully. "Just have to take both," he said to himself. He stood and turned to Grennel. "I need the legs," he said. "And the head, too, for the control circuitry. Can we hack them off, as cleanly as possible?"

Grennel unsheathed his hunting knife, bent down, and impossibly fast, leveraging his weight against the blade, with a few grunts of effort he removed the legs and head from the torso. He sheathed his knife, picked up the legs, and tossed them to Wynn, who caught them neatly. Then he grabbed the head and tossed it to Wynn, who quickly shifted both legs under her right arm and caught it with her left hand. She grinned. Kevin felt vaguely sickened.

On the short walk to the supply shed Kevin saw four more human bodies, but no more bots. One of the bodies was small, definitely not an adult. Kevin didn't look closely. He didn't want to know.

The door of the supply shed was crumpled and lying on the ground, and the contents of the building were in disarray—most of the equipment was on the floor, in jumbled heaps. Kevin picked through the mess, not sure what he was hoping to find. He needed something to help him solve the puzzle of the camouflage suits, but he didn't know what that thing might be. Nothing he found helped. Basic circuitry, conduction wire clamps, some cracked and shattered vidscreens—useless. He found a few tools that might help his tinkering—a nano-solder, a set of scope glasses that had miraculously survived intact—but nothing else. He nodded at Grennel, who was watching him from the entrance. "Done," he said, pocketing the few tools he had scavenged.

Grennel held out his hand. "I'll hold the tools," he said.

"What am I going to do, use my scope glasses to look you to death?" said Kevin.

"I recall a report of your misuse of a nanosolder not long ago," said Grennel, still holding out his hand. "You can have them when we return to the camp."

Kevin scowled, annoyed, but he handed over the tools. He pushed past Grennel and headed toward his grandfather's workshop. This trip was starting to look like a big mistake. The Island was nothing but an open graveyard now; he didn't think he was going to find anything to help him with the camouflage suits, and judging by the complexity of the little he had seen of the bot leg circuitry, he wasn't going to be able to do much with them to help Farryn. What had he been thinking? His grandfather had been a genius; he was just a kid who had been taught to tinker with power grids by his dead friend Tom. He trudged forward in silence.

And then they had to step past two more bodies lying in the path, a man and a woman. The woman's head lay on the man's stomach, faceup, like they were a couple taking a nap after a picnic . . . except for the blood, and the unblinking eyes, and the frozen look of agony on their faces. Kevin quickly stopped feeling sorry for himself. He was alive. His family was alive.

They were in trouble, no doubt, but they were alive, and for that, he realized, he should be grateful.

The door to the workshop was intact, and open. Grennel descended first. Kevin hesitated. This was where his grandfather had been lased. By the man he was about to follow down the stairs.

Wynn pushed him on the shoulder, and Kevin took a deep breath and walked down into the workshop. The underground room was dimly lit by the light coming in from the door; Grennel flared a lightstick from his pack and the room lit up.

His grandfather wasn't there.

The Island survivor had been right—perhaps the City bots had taken the body away.

Grennel handed him another lightstick. "Search quickly," he said.

Kevin grabbed the light. What could he say, to the man who had killed his grandfather, in the very room where the murder had taken place? "Go to hell," he said.

Grennel raised his eyebrows, and Wynn took a step toward Kevin, but Grennel looked at her and shook his head. She stopped.

Kevin swallowed his anger and began to look around the room. It looked to have been swept through—his grandfather's tools were missing, and the drawers from the worktables were open and bare. Kevin moved through the room slowly, shining his lightstrip to banish the shadows. What was he looking for?

He didn't know. Would he even know it if he saw it? Would the City bots have possibly left anything useful behind? He *needed* to find something useful—Clay wasn't going to be happy if he came back empty-handed. . . .

His hopes grew dimmer as he continued to scan the room, finding absolutely nothing. He stood staring at the control box from which the Wall control unit had been taken. He shined his light on the empty chamber, and the thick conduction wires snaking away from the chamber in eight directions. Nothing. The room had been picked clean. He looked down at the floor, at the spot where his grandfather had fallen, lased in the back. Was there blood? A mark of some sort? No, the floor was untouched. There was nothing to indicate that a man had died on this very spot.

He turned to go, but something caught his eye and made him stop. The conduction wires. The clamps that held them to the wall. He stepped closer, shining the light directly on one of the clamps, and felt a prickle of excitement in his fingertips. It had a small switch on it, and two recessed buttons, and, most interesting, a very small vidscreen, no larger than a thumbnail, currently black.

Kevin began feeling all around the clamp, hoping . . . and yes . . . he was right . . . he could feel small wiring, extending into the conduction wire. He yanked on the clamp, which didn't move, and chided himself for acting like an idiot. He examined it even more closely, and then he found it, a tiny trigger that opened with a hard tug of his pointer finger. The clamp fell into his hands. Kevin studied the circuit wires, the two sets, one that had to be a control set, the other most likely a ground of some sort. . . .

He wasn't sure, but he would bet that these clamps were energy modulators. It made sense, from an engineering perspective. It seemed a bit old-fashioned, but it would be an easy way for his grandfather to adjust the various flows of his Wall grid. He had been working in the wilderness; he probably didn't have the material for anything more elegant. He had used leather on his bots, after all.

"I've got it," said Kevin over his shoulder, without looking back. "This is it." He carefully unclamped the rest of the modulators, setting them one by one on the floor. He picked one up and began to study it. First he'd have to adapt them for portable use . . . and of course he'd have to figure out how to split the energy feeds . . . maybe there'd be some way to broadcast the field? He could adapt some of the rebels' comm units . . . yes, that was an interesting idea. . . .

Grennel stepped forward and took the clamp from Kevin's hand. Kevin, lost in his thoughts, was startled. Grennel bent down and picked up the other seven clamps, and placed them all in his pack. "Let's go," he said.

Kevin turned toward the stairs, and then the flash of his lightstrip glinted on something under his grandfather's worktable. Kevin bent down, aiming the light, and found, deep under the table, a small vid. He got down on his belly and reached, his arm scraping painfully against the table edge, and retrieved the vid. He looked down at it, and felt his stomach twist. He knew what this was. He tapped the power, half expecting it to be broken, but it glowed into life, showing a still of his grandfather, from years ago, standing next to his father. He stared at it a moment, then flicked the vid off.

"This is mine," he said to Grennel. "This is my family's. You can't have this." He was expecting Grennel to take it anyway, but Grennel surprised him by nodding.

"Very well," he said. "Keep it."

Back out in the sunlight and fresh air, Kevin took a deep breath, then carefully stashed the photo vid in his pack. He followed Grennel down the path, toward the Island gates. As they passed the two bodies on the path, the man and woman, Grennel paused, looking down at them, then bent down, and with a casual show of impressive strength, picked up one of the corpses, the man, and heaved it over his shoulder. "Get the woman," he said to Wynn.

"Why?" she said.

"Do it," said Grennel. "We may not have time to bury them, but a pyre is quick."

So Grennel and Wynn spent twenty minutes gathering bodies into a pile near the mess hall. Kevin helped, too, dragging one Islander by the feet. It was the most horrifying thing he had ever had to do. They found twelve bodies—Kevin was sure there were more, buried under the collapsed buildings, but there was no time for digging. Grennel laid them side by side, on a pile of lumber. "Back," he said, and both Wynn and Kevin moved away from the pyre. Grennel set a lightstrip on top of the bodies, stepped away, and then released a full burst from his rifle. It hit the lightstrip, and the small power source from the strip exploded as it melted, amplifying the explosion. The pyre flared into flames.

Grennel and Wynn and Kevin watched the pyre burn for a quiet minute, black smoke rising into the sky, the flames initially flaring green from the chemicals in the lightstrip, then settling back into red and orange. As the fire roared and crackled, they turned their backs on the Island and toward the setting sun.

CHAPTER 13

NICK SAT NEAR ERICA, WATCHING HER AS SHE ATE A CHARRED PIECE OF
squirrel meat for dinner. He had been guarding her for most
of the day. It was a pointless assignment—she couldn't go
beyond the posts that would trigger her shock collar. And she
was refusing to speak to him. He had given up on trying to
make conversation hours ago, so the two of them just sat, Erica
inside her shock perimeter, Nick outside.

"You need anything?" he asked. "More food? I can probably find you a blanket or maybe even a pad. . . ."

Erica shook her head. She tossed the squirrel bone into
the firepit and wiped her hand on her pants. Nick noticed
that she was favoring the leg that held the reimplanted chip.
She must be hurting, he knew. That leg had been gouged

into twice in a matter of days. He winced inwardly at the thought.

"I'm responsible for you," he said.

"No, you're not," Erica said. It was the most she had said to him in hours.

"General told me I am," Nick replied.

Erica stared at Nick, then took two limping steps toward him. She stopped just shy of the shock perimeter. "What do you want, Nick? A thank-you?"

"I just want to make sure you're going to be okay," Nick said angrily. He hadn't been fishing for a thank-you, but still, he didn't think he deserved the hostility. If not for him, she would be dead.

"Never better," said Erica.

"Yeah, well, fine," Nick said, and he turned away. No point forcing a conversation.

"Nick, wait," Erica said, her voice softening just a touch.

Nick stopped and turned back to face her.

"I meant what I said before," she said. "About not being responsible for you, or Cass, or Lexi." She hesitated, and it looked like she wanted to say more, so Nick said nothing and waited. "I've already let the bots blackmail me," she continued quietly. "And I know that was a mistake."

"How many people did you betray, trying to protect your family?" said Nick quietly. He was surprised how little anger he felt. More than anything else, it just made him sad.

A flash of anger showed on Erica's face. "Haven't we been over this?" she said. "I was doing what I thought was necessary to keep my brother alive. You would have done the same."

"No," said Nick. *Maybe*, he thought.

"Come here," Erica said.

He took a step toward her.

"Closer," Erica said. Nick hesitated, then stepped inside the shock collar perimeter. Erica walked up to him. She leaned forward, putting her mouth close to his ear, and Nick's breath caught in his throat. "When the bots find out I'm giving them false info, they're going to kill my brother," she whispered. "I have to find a way to save him."

"Why are you telling me this?" Nick whispered back, his lips nearly touching her ear.

"So you know, when I'm gone."

Nick began to step away, but Erica put a hand on his cheek, pulled him back close, and kissed him on the neck. Her lips were soft and warm, and her body pressed against his briefly, before she stepped back. He just stood there, speechless.

Rabbit came up the path toward them, and Nick quickly moved out of the shock perimeter. He saw Rabbit not-so-subtly shift his hand closer to his right hip, where he had a lase pistol holstered.

"Relax, Rabbit," Nick said.

Rabbit kept his hand close to his gun as he closed the distance between them. "My shift," he said. "Be back here at sunrise."

Erica spun to face Rabbit, her smile turning into scorn. "You just follow orders, don't you, Rabbit?" she said.

"That's right," said Rabbit.

"Just like a good bot," she said.

Rabbit chuckled humorlessly. He put his hand on the grip of his pistol. "Would you prefer I ignore my orders, and go ahead and execute you myself? Because I'd love to."

Nick took a step toward Rabbit. . . . Would he be able to reach the man before he could get a shot off? Rabbit grinned, and pulled the pistol halfway out of the holster.

Nick glared at Rabbit, waiting long enough to show he wasn't scared, then turned to Erica. "I'll see you in the morning," he said, then walked away.

CHAPTER 14

THEY HIKED BACK FROM THE ISLAND IN NEAR-TOTAL SILENCE. GRENNEL and Wynn were tight-lipped as usual, and Kevin found he didn't have much to say, or any desire to break the quiet. So he walked without speaking, in the light of the bright full moon, treading the near-silent walk of someone who had lived his entire life in the forest. Grennel hiked just as quietly, and Kevin wondered where Grennel had learned his skills. Wynn made only a touch more noise—an occasional crack of a twig or rustle of leaves.

Kevin thought about the black smoke rising from the funeral pyre, how thick it had been, and about his grandfather— had the bots really taken his body away? When they paused for a few hours of rest, in his fitful sleep he dreamed about the twisted bodies of the Islanders.

In the morning when they approached the camp, it was Oswald who was covering the eastern guard point. He stepped out from behind a thick tree and raised his hand in greeting. Kevin, lost in his thoughts, was startled, but Grennel and Wynn, he saw with embarrassment, had seen Oswald in advance.

"Welcome back," said Oswald. "General's been waiting for you. Told me to keep an eye out for you and tell you to report immediately."

Grennel nodded. "The Islander. You delivered him safely?"

Oswald hesitated. "You'll have to talk to the General about that."

Faster than Kevin thought was possible—the movement was just a blur—Grennel rushed forward, grabbed Oswald's throat, stepped one leg behind him, and pushed him backward. Grennel pressed his pistol against Oswald's cheek. Oswald's eyes were wide with shock, but he stayed still and said nothing.

"I told you what would happen if you did not deliver the man safely," Grennel said.

"I got him here fine," Oswald whispered, half-choked. "After that it was General's orders."

Kevin could see the open anger on Grennel's face, and it shocked him. The man never showed emotion. Grennel continued to hold Oswald down, pressing the pistol into his face, and Kevin thought, *He's going to shoot him, or choke him to death. I'm going to watch Oswald die.* But then Grennel's face calmed, and he released Oswald's throat.

Oswald slowly got to his feet, coughing and rubbing his neck. Grennel strode past him, forcing Oswald to move quickly to get out of his way. Kevin followed, looking at Oswald, still holding his hand up to his chest as he walked past.

"What the hell are you looking at, boy?" growled Oswald. He moved his hand from his throat to the butt of his pistol. Kevin looked away, trying to not do it too quickly—he didn't want Oswald to think he could be scared that easily.

"Wynn, you're dismissed," Grennel said as he entered the camp. "Kevin, come with me." Grennel triggered his comm bracelet. "General, Grennel reporting in."

Kevin was relieved to see Cass sitting against a tree outside Clay's tent. She jumped up and gave Kevin a big hug. "It's good to see you," she said. She took a deep breath, then let it out and smiled. "I was worried."

"What are you doing here?" said Kevin. He could still feel his heart beating fast from Grennel and Oswald's violent encounter.

Cass's smile dropped into a frown. "Waiting on the General. She's made me her rusted servant."

Kevin felt a twinge of anxiety. "That's not good," he said. "You should stay away from her."

"Where am I going to go?" said Cass.

Kevin didn't say anything. She was right.

The tent flap opened and Clay stepped out. She nodded at Grennel. "Welcome back," she said. She glanced at Cass. "Cass, you're done for the day. Grennel and Kevin, in my tent."

Cass gave Kevin's arm a quick squeeze. "Find me later," she whispered. She walked away.

Clay stood inside her tent, hands on her hips. "Report," she said. "Were you successful?" She looked at Kevin. "Or did you waste my time? I sincerely hope not."

"The man," said Grennel. "The Islander that we found, that I had Oswald bring back. What happened to him?"

Clay raised her eyebrows. "I asked you to report."

Grennel clenched his jaw—Kevin could see the muscles on his face tightening—and then he said, "We returned to the Island. Kevin recovered tools from the supply shed, as well as hardware from the Governor's workshop that he believes will be useful. And we came across an Islander, lost in the woods. I had Oswald bring him to the camp."

"He was a spy," said Clay. "I had him quietly removed."

"He was no spy," said Grennel.

"Enough!" said Clay. "I don't expect this from you, Grennel," she said, lowering her voice. "You're disappointing me."

Grennel said nothing. His arms were crossed over his chest. Kevin tried not to breathe.

"He was an Islander and I was not willing to risk him undermining my authority. Understood?"

Grennel was quiet a moment longer, while Clay glared at him, and then he lowered his arms and nodded, anger still obvious on his face.

"Anything else to report?" Clay said. Grennel shook his head. Kevin was surprised—he hadn't mentioned the parts salvaged from the bot, or the photo vid.

Clay held her stare a few more long moments, then turned to Kevin. "Tell me what you found," she said.

Kevin had to fight the mix of anger and anxiety that he felt whenever Clay spoke to him. "The clamps of the conduction wires can be used to modulate the energy flow. I think I can adapt them to use on the suits and make it safe."

Clay frowned and waved him to be quiet. "Enough," she said. "Get back to work. Two days, and you will be inside a suit, testing it. It is up to you whether or not you fry like that fool Stebbins. Understood?"

I'd like to fry you, he thought. But he just nodded. "Got it," he said.

CHAPTER 15

CASS WATCHED CLAY AND GRENNEL DISAPPEAR INTO THE WOODS. THEY
had left at the same time the past three mornings, and had been
gone until lunchtime. She waited another minute, to be sure,
and then she ducked into Clay's tent. She had a half-formed
plan to steal Clay's vid, have Kevin or Farryn hack into it, find
out what she could, then get it back before Clay returned.

Her heart was thumping as she looked around Clay's tent
for the vid. *One hour*, she told herself. No more than one hour,
and then she'd have the vid back, in exactly the same spot she
had found it. Clay would never know. She looked under the
pillow first, but it wasn't there. She tried the trunk next to
the bed, inside a duffel bag, the space between the cot and
the tent—nothing. Clay must have taken it with her, she

realized—she was taking this huge risk for nothing—and then she lifted Clay's mattress and there it was.

Cass carefully picked up the vid and set the mattress back down.

The tent flap opened, and Clay and Grennel stepped inside.

Cass just stood there like an idiot, frozen with the vid in her hands. *Move*, she told herself. *Do something. Say something.* "It's not . . . I'm not . . ." she began weakly.

Clay took her pistol out of its holster at her hip, and aimed it at Cass. "Grennel, leave us," she said.

Cass took a step back, and lifted up her hands. *I'm going to die now*, she realized. *Do I dive behind the cot? Throw the vid at Clay?*

"General . . ." said Grennel.

"Go," growled Clay, her eyes, and gun, still trained on Cass.

"She's just a child," said Grennel.

"I said go!" said Clay.

Grennel left the tent.

"So, Cass," Clay said, waving at the vid with her gun. "Tidying up the tent for me?"

Cass didn't say anything. She would throw the vid at Clay, and duck to the left, she decided. If Clay's shot missed, maybe she'd somehow be able to get past her and out of the tent and then just run, as fast as she could.

"Put the vid down on the bed," Clay said. "And tell me what you were doing."

Cass hesitated, then dropped the vid onto the cot. She tried to come up with a plausible lie, her mind spinning frantically, then decided, *The hell with it.* "I wanted to find out what I could about your plans," she said.

"To report back to the bots? To other True Believers?"

"No!" said Cass.

"Then why?" said Clay.

"Because it seems crazy, to attack a City," Cass said. The words began to tumble out. "Because Kevin hates you and is scared to death of you and I trust him. Because I don't trust you and I want to know what you're doing before you lead us all on some suicide mission. Because it seems like you hate True Believers as much as bots and I want to know if you're going to kill my parents." Cass was breathing hard, fighting back tears.

Clay smiled, her horrible thin grimace. "If killing your parents brings us closer to defeating the bots, then I'll do it in a heartbeat," she said. She pointed at a chair. "Sit down. Don't move."

Cass sat. Clay quickly crossed the distance between them, and Cass put her hands up, thinking Clay was going to hit her, but instead she grabbed the vid off the cot, then quickly stepped back. She holstered her gun, and Cass felt a rush of relief, but Clay was still blocking the exit.

"My entire battalion, except for me and Grennel and a few damned traitors, were killed by the bots," Clay said. "My husband was killed. My parents were killed. Even my god-damned rusted cat, blown up by the bots." She flicked on the vid, and tapped in a password, then began reading.

"Rebel unit one. Approx. fifty fighters. Handheld burst weapons, no heavy artillery. Trained medic. Group commander: Ro." She looked up at Cass. "That's us," she said. "Here. Now." She looked back down at the vid, and tapped on it angrily. "Island. Neutralized. Assets extracted." She tapped again. "Northeast, three miles, rebel unit three. Approx. forty fighters. Handheld burst weapons, one small-scale mobile burst cannon. Group commander: Helena, ex-military asset, but potentially too ambitious." She waved the vid at Cass. "What else do you want to know?"

Cass shook her head.

"The City," Clay said. "Your True Believer parents. You want to know about that?" She read from her vid. "Bot-controlled, City 73. Medium-size metropolitan, construction both pre-Rev and new. Limited air and ground defense. Bot numbers unknown, but max of five hundred. Majority of human population re-educated loyal True Believers. Viable quick-strike target when Island tech is online." She tapped again on the screen, then waved the vid at Cass, showing her a brief glimpse of what appeared to be a map of the City. "I've even got City layouts. I know what we need to hit, and how fast."

Clay turned off the vid and threw it onto the bed. She took

a step toward Cass, who instinctively jumped out of her chair and backed away.

"Sit down," Clay said.

Cass didn't move.

"I said *sit down*," Clay said.

Cass sat, her hands gripping the edge of the cot, ready to move if Clay came at her.

"Don't question me, Cass," said Clay. "I've been working on this for years. I have rebels all over these woods. I'm going to beat these bots or die trying and I'll kill anyone who interferes with my plans." She lowered her voice to a near-whisper and bent down toward Cass's face. "I'm a leader, Cass. I decide. I act. I keep the primary objective of the mission paramount, and I don't get distracted by tangential details or collateral damage. Tell your brothers what I've told you today. Tell anyone you want." She straightened back up. "And I swear, Cass, I'll kill you if you ever set foot in my tent again without permission. Understood?"

Cass nodded carefully.

"Get out," Clay said.

Cass jumped up and hurried out of the tent, not giving Clay a chance to change her mind.

CHAPTER 16

THE SENIOR ADVISOR STOOD OVER THE METAL TABLE AND LOOKED DOWN at Dr. Winston. The man lay on the cold metal slab in a brown jumpsuit, breathing shallowly. His wrists were strapped to the table, yet his hands still trembled. A cough wracked his body and he turned his head to the side to spit a mixture of phlegm and blood. The Senior Advisor continued to watch him.

"What now?" Dr. Winston said, his voice a hoarse rasp.

"Robots do not feel pain, as you of course know," said the Senior Advisor. "We receive constant feedback on our system status, and are aware if we have received any damage, or are malfunctioning." The Senior Advisor shrugged—another gesture he had been practicing. "Unless of course the damage has compromised our system status feedback loop." He reached down and pressed a pale finger into the swollen, black-and-blue area under Dr. Winston's right eye. The doctor winced, and weakly turned his head away. The Senior Advisor pulled his hand back. "But we do not feel pain as you humans do. Can you describe pain? What is it, exactly, to feel?"

Dr. Winston said nothing, and the Senior Advisor nodded. "No, of course not. Pain simply is . . ." The Senior Advisor hesitated. "An intrinsic human quality. Inexplicable because it is part of the essence of being human, am I correct?"

Dr. Winston coughed again. "What is your point?" he said.

The Senior Advisor smiled, a gesture that moved his lips without touching the rest of his face. "We are simply having a conversation."

"Just let me die," Dr. Winston said.

The Senior Advisor shook his head. "No," he said. He touched Dr. Winston's chest, and released a small burst of energy. Dr. Winston screamed and arched his back, his fingers clawing at the table. The Senior Advisor held the contact, and Dr. Winston continued to writhe and moan. Finally the Senior Advisor pulled away, letting Dr. Winston collapse back to the metal slab, panting. Tears ran down his cheeks.

"You are elderly, and your body is frail, but we are monitoring your biofeedback carefully," said the Senior Advisor. "You will be able to suffer a great deal, but we will not kill you." He leaned forward, and set his hand on Dr. Winston's shoulder. The Doctor flinched at the touch, but the Senior Advisor did not generate any energy with the connection this time. "Of course, you can spare yourself from this pain—which apparently is extremely unpleasant—if you help us bypass the replication blocking code."

"I've already told you, it's a failsafe that can't be bypassed," said Dr. Winston, between quick, shallow breaths. "I wasn't even the designer of that code."

"I think you are being too humble," said the Senior Advisor. "You, more than any other human, are responsible for creating us. You designed me, after all. I think you can find a way around the code."

"It can't be done," said Dr. Winston. And then he turned his head and looked directly at the Senior Advisor. "And I wouldn't help you rebuild yourselves even if I could. I helped build you once, and it has been . . ." Dr. Winston paused, to catch his breath. "It has been the deepest shame imaginable. I will not compound that mistake."

The Senior Advisor shrugged again, this time using the other shoulder. He had not yet decided which shoulder was preferable—humans seemed to use both almost equally. "Well, Father, we will see if more carefully administered pain changes your mind. And if not, then we'll have to find stronger incentive."

CHAPTER 17

KEVIN HAD STAYED UP MOST OF THE NIGHT WIRING THE CLAMPS HE HAD scavenged from his grandfather's lab. It was more guesswork than he would have liked—but he was afraid to burn out another clamp. He had seven left, and he planned on using all of them.

In the morning he left the unit on for thirty seconds, forcing himself to count the time slowly. If it overloaded, not only would it ruin the clamp, it might go off like a bomb. He hit thirty in his head, and flicked the unit off, his heart pounding. The gear cloaked perfectly, disappearing from the table, then reappearing, undamaged, when he turned the unit off.

Next, he pulled apart a comm bracelet, grabbing the broadcasting and retrieving chipsets. This part was pure speculation—he rigged up the broadcast to the Wall unit, and looped the receiver into the circuit of the clamp he had set up on the camouflage unit. His hunch had better be correct, otherwise the camouflaged soldiers would have to be walking around in a closed-circuit, wired clump, tripping all over one another. Kind of a funny idea, Kevin thought, but he knew Clay didn't have a sense of humor.

It probably wouldn't be very efficient—if the broadcast worked at all the energy leakage would be pretty substantial—but he was cloaking a person, not a huge, mile-perimeter wall. Of course, he didn't fully understand the nature of the energy that would be leaking out, but he couldn't worry about that. If he got a headache, or a nosebleed, or if eggs started frying in their shells, he'd dial things down.

The first time he tried to broadcast the energy flow, the vest flickered, like he was looking at it through foggy glasses, but didn't disappear. "Damn," he muttered, his heart sinking, and then he mentally kicked himself. Of course. The leakage. Less energy was coming through, so he had to adjust the clamp, which was still set to cut out almost all the energy. He dialed the clamp back and this time the vest became almost invisible, but when he squinted, he could still make out the ghostly outline. He cranked down the clamp a bit more and tried again. The vest disappeared.

The next step was a bit more dicey, Kevin knew, but it had to be done. He placed his left arm carefully inside the sleeve of the vest he had wired. He stretched the rest of his body as far away from the unit as possible, and braced himself. If he started to feel any pain, he'd pull his arm out right away. It should be fine—unless of course the energy somehow fried his arm instantly.

That's why he was using his left arm. He was right-handed.

He took a deep breath, held it, gritted his teeth, and turned on the unit. The vest, and his arm, disappeared. There was no pain. He waited . . . still nothing. He unclenched his jaw, and let himself breathe. It was an amazing experience—he could feel his arm, he knew it was there, but looking down at where it should be, there was nothing. He switched the unit off, and the vest, and his arm, reappeared. He looked at his hand, wiggled his fingers, and grinned.

When Clay and Grennel arrived later that morning, Kevin was already almost done wiring a second unit. His heart started thumping hard when he saw Clay approaching, but he forced himself to keep working, to pretend he didn't care about her arrival. Damned if he was ever going to show Clay any fear.

"Well?" Clay said. She stood above him, hands on her hips. Grennel towered over her in the background.

"Oh, hey, didn't notice you," said Kevin, setting his tools down. "Came by to say hello?"

"I came by to see you disappear," said Clay. "Now. No more waiting."

Kevin stood up. "No problem," he said. He slipped on the camouflage vest. "You might want to stand back a bit," he said, gesturing with his hand. He smiled at Clay. "In case I blow up."

Clay crossed her arms over her chest, but took two steps back.

Kevin double-checked the dampen setting. It was set properly. He tried not to look nervous, to let Clay see that his heart was about to pound out of his chest. Despite Kevin's testing, he couldn't help but be worried. The last time this had been tried, Stebbins had ended up dead.

"There are still a number of details I haven't worked out," he said. "I haven't tested the range, and once we have multiple suits working at the same time, I'll probably have to adjust the modulation since they'll be drawing more energy. And I don't know if it's safe long-term. . . . I haven't tested it for more than thirty seconds—"

"Enough stalling," Clay cut him off. "Turn it on."

Feeling dizzy from anxiety, Kevin reached over and flicked on the power to the unit. His sight flickered for a moment, like he had just stepped through smoke, then cleared. He held his hand up to his face, and his heart sank. His hand was visible, clear as day. He opened his mouth, to explain, somehow, although he had no idea what had gone wrong . . . but then he realized that Clay was grinning, and Grennel looked relieved.

"Ha!" said Clay, clapping her hands together once. "You did it!"

Kevin felt a flood of relief. *Interesting*, he thought. From within the field, his body was visible to himself. . . . That was useful, actually.

Kevin took five silent steps to his left, and sure enough, Clay continued to look at the spot where he had been. "Good," she said. "Very good! Turn off the camouflage now." Kevin flipped off the power, and Clay spun to look at him.

Kevin felt exultant. He had done it. He had a crazy thought . . . to pick up the Wall unit and get his brother and sister and City friends and just walk out of the camp, just keep walking, invisible, as far away from Clay as possible.

"Congratulations," she said. "Well done. You live to see another day."

Kevin took off the vest and set it on the table. Clay stepped forward and touched it, examining the clamp and wiring. "You have eight of these, you said? How quickly can you make the rest?"

"Two days. But I only have six," Kevin said. "Two were destroyed in testing." Clay studied his face, and he held her gaze. *Stay calm*, he told himself. *She can't know you're lying, unless you give it away like a baby. . . .*

Clay nodded and looked away, and Kevin had to hold back a sigh of relief. "Very well," she said. "Finish the rest of the suits. Test the range, and tune the . . . what was it . . . the modulation, you said? You have two days."

CHAPTER 18

THE WORD FILTERED DOWN THROUGH THE REBELS TO NICK—THE GENERAL
was ready to attack City 73. Two days, and they'd be on the
march. A quick, strategic attack on the City, scavenge supplies,
gather new recruits from rescued City folk, then on to the next
City. Everyone was going about their business with a new
intensity and focus. Ro strode through the campsite like a drill
sergeant, finding excuses to get angry and assign extra work.

Nick remained stuck guarding the still-silent Erica. He needed
to be part of the attack. He needed to get back into the City and
find his parents. He couldn't be trapped on the sidelines.

His problems were solved at the next guard shift. Rabbit
appeared at sundown to relieve him, which Nick was expecting, but with Rabbit was Grennel, and another rebel whom

Nick didn't know, a tall, tan, bald-headed man. All three men were carrying backpacks.

"It's time for your transmission," Grennel said to Erica. "Activate your leg comm, and tell the bots that you have intel that indicates that there will be an attack on City 68 in two days. Say anything else and we will be forced to shoot you." He nodded at Rabbit and the other man, who aimed their burst rifles at Erica.

Nick watched Erica press on her leg in a staccato pattern with her forefinger, then quietly repeat Grennel's message, then tap on her leg again. "Done," Erica said.

Grennel nodded. "You'll be heading toward City 68 with Rabbit and Moss as guards. A decoy for the bots. You'll continue to wear your shock collar, and if you cause any trouble, Rabbit or Moss will kill you." Moss nodded solemnly, and Rabbit grinned.

"When do I leave?" Erica said.

"Now," said Grennel. He unslung his backpack and tossed it to Erica, who caught it smoothly.

"Nick, you're done here," said Grennel.

Nick looked at Erica, who met his gaze and wouldn't look away. His thoughts about her were so confused he didn't know where to begin. She had betrayed them to the bots. He should hate her. But she had been trying to save her family. He thought of Erica's dark eyes, her confident smile, her bravery, her warm lips on his neck. . . .

"Good luck," he said, the words sounding weak and insufficient to his own ears.

Erica looked at him a moment longer, then nodded and turned away. Rabbit and Jack led her into the woods.

He watched her disappear, then hurried off to find Kevin. Nick found him in his usual spot, bent over one of the black vests that he had been working on frantically for the past few days. Kevin was carefully adjusting the wiring on one of the salvaged clamps that he had attached to the side of the vest, and didn't even look up as Nick approached.

"You should pay more attention," Nick said. "Shouldn't let people sneak up on you."

"You didn't sneak up on me," Kevin said. "I heard you. I just didn't bother to look up."

"I could have been anyone," Nick said.

Kevin set down his tools and finally looked up at Nick. "Nah," he said, smiling, "I'm downwind of you. I'd recognize your smell anywhere."

Nick laughed, despite himself. "Smelled yourself recently?" he said.

Kevin shrugged. "No time," he said. "Been working too hard on these vests."

"How's it going?" said Nick. "And what the heck are you doing, anyway? I want to help—the camp's been buzzing about some secret weapon that Clay's got, and I'm guessing that means you."

Kevin stood and slipped on the vest he had been tinkering with. "Watch this," he said with a smile. He reached over to a black box that was resting on the ground next to his left foot, flipped a switch, and disappeared.

Nick froze, then took a step toward where Kevin had been. "What the . . ." he began, and then he heard Kevin's laughter, off to his left. The switch on the control box flipped, seemingly by itself, and Kevin reappeared, for a moment just a ghostly shadow, then quickly growing more substantial, until after a few seconds he stood there, completely solid and visible again, a few paces to the left of where he had vanished.

"What did you do?" Nick said, so surprised he could barely get the words out.

"It's our grandfather's tech," Kevin said, stepping close to Nick so he could speak quietly. "I adapted it for Clay, after she stole it." He looked away for a moment, and Nick could see that Kevin was struggling with something private, so he waited quietly. After a moment Kevin continued. "I made it work," he said. "I don't think Clay thought I could do it. She was looking forward to watching me fry." His voice was an odd mix of pride and anger.

"But you did it," Nick said.

Kevin swiped angrily at his eyes with the back of his sleeve. "Six camo suits, with a wireless range of a half mile from the generator."

With a jolt, Nick understood why Ro, and the camp, was so

on edge. With his brother's tech, Clay would be able to launch a quick strike on City 73. He felt a rush of excitement, mixed with queasy nerves. This would be a chance to fight. To do something. Hopefully to save their parents.

Kevin leaned closer and whispered, "I told her I have six suits, but I made a seventh. One got destroyed." He took a quick glance around, then continued, "I'll be wearing the extra one myself, to get into the City and find Mom and Dad."

Nick thought of his brother, picking his way through the chaos of a battle, carrying a blast rifle that was practically bigger than him. "That's crazy," he said. "You don't even know how to use a gun."

"You point it and pull the trigger," said Kevin. He folded his arms over his chest. "It's *my* suit. I'll do what I want."

"You're not a fighter," Nick said. And then, even though he knew it wasn't going to go well, he said, "Let me use the extra suit."

"Right, because you've got to be the hero," Kevin said bitterly. "Can't stand the idea of your kid brother getting any glory. I shouldn't even have told you."

"To hell with the damned glory!" said Nick, too loudly. He lowered his voice. "I just don't want you to get killed."

"I'll be invisible, Nick," said Kevin. "As in, the bots won't be able to see me."

"A lucky blast will still kill you, even if they can't see you," said Nick. "And do you really know the suits are going to work?

How much have you tested them? And how are you going to find Mom and Dad? And how are you going to get them out even if you do find them?"

"I'll improvise," Kevin said.

"Damn it, Kevin," Nick said, starting to feel helpless. What would he have to do to keep Kevin out of the battle? Steal the extra camo suit? Tie him to a tree?

Kevin surprised Nick by answering calmly, gently almost. "It'll be okay," he said. "I got this."

Nick stared down at his brother, then shook his head and put his hand on Kevin's shoulder. "I hope you're right," he said quietly.

Kevin smiled. "In any case, it's going to be pretty damned fletch."

CHAPTER 19

CASS WAS PUT TO WORK ORGANIZING AND PACKING SUPPLIES FOR THE hike to City 73. The camp was buzzing with nervous energy. Clay herself was full of barely contained excitement, flashing that shark smile of hers, with a bounce in her step and extra spring to her stride as she rushed around the campsite.

It seemed like suicide to attack the bots head-on, even if Clay brought together her other units from the area, but there was buzz among the rebels of some sort of sneak attack that would cripple the City's defenses. And then she had heard from Nick about Kevin's camouflage vests, and it all made sense. If they could just walk right in, unseen, even only six fighters—they could wreak havoc and the City would probably be wide open to the rest of Clay's forces.

City 73. The City where her parents were being held. Where her birth parents and her sister, Penny, lived. It had to be. It was a good thing, Cass told herself, a chance to fight back against the bots and rescue her families—but she pictured the City as a war zone, and felt more dread than excitement. The tall buildings of Hightown reduced to rubble. Lexi's neighborhood burning. Doc's apartment razed. Would all the people she wanted to save even survive the rescue?

And then of course there was Clay. She didn't see the fight as a rescue, Cass was certain of that. She'd be just as happy to kill people she considered True Believers as she would be to destroy bots.

Cass stuffed the final energy paste pack into a backpack, took a deep breath, and stood up tall. She felt a sharp moment of fear, a twisting in her belly, but she pushed it away. She knew what she had to do. She had known all along, really.

She went off to find Farryn. She couldn't tell her brothers—they would try to stop her. But she had to tell someone, and besides, she wanted to say good-bye.

When Cass found Farryn, she stopped dead in her tracks, momentarily forgetting what she had come to say. Farryn saw her and grinned—almost his usual smile, but mixed with a touch of shyness that made her heart thump extra hard.

He stood next to the firepit. Without crutches.

On two legs.

He was wearing long green canvas pants, and two boots,

and Cass felt a dizzy, illogical panic—was her memory still broken? Had she imagined his injury and the amputation? Had the last week not even been real?

And then he walked toward her, awkwardly stiff, his right leg unbending, and Cass thought, *Of course. The bot leg.*

"What do you think?" he said. "Almost as good as new, right?"

Cass forced herself to smile, although she was still fighting off her disorientation. "Amazing!" she said. "What did you . . . I mean, what is . . ." She struggled for the right words, feeling her cheeks starting to burn.

"Kevin's leg," Farryn said. "The one he found for me. I set up some straps, a ball-and-socket joint. . . . There was no way I was going to manage any neurological connections, Kevin was just dreaming about that, so it's really just a high-tech stump."

"It's great," Cass said.

"You think?" Farryn said. "It's not . . . it doesn't look too strange?" He was all shyness and vulnerability, and Cass felt a tightness in her throat. She just wanted to hug him.

"It's wonderful," she said. "It's like you grew your leg back." *Idiot!* she thought. *What a horrible thing to say!* But Farryn smiled, a genuine, happy smile, and she relaxed, and found herself smiling back.

And then she remembered why she had come, and her happiness died away. Farryn frowned. "What is it?" he said.

Cass glanced around; nobody else was within earshot. "I'm going back to the City."

Farryn's face fell. It looked like he had been shot. Cass felt terrible for doing that to him, but she also felt a crackle of nerves in her fingers and the back of her neck. *He really does care about me*, she realized.

"What are you talking about?" he whispered urgently. "But your memory came back . . . you beat the re-education, Cass. . . ."

She touched his arm. "No, you don't understand. I'm sorry, I'm explaining this like an idiot." She paused, took a deep breath, then started over. "You've heard Clay is going to attack the City, right?"

Farryn nodded, his face still pale.

"It's going to be my chance to save my birth parents, and my sister. Nick isn't going to help them, and Clay might end up killing them, so it's up to me."

Farryn was quiet for a moment, then he nodded. "Okay. I'm going with you."

Cass was caught off guard. The thought of not having to do this alone, and that Farryn would again risk everything for her, made her warm with happiness and relief, but then she got mad at herself, and at Farryn. "It's my family," she said. "I'm not some weak little girl who needs babysitting."

"Believe me, I know," Farryn said, grinning, putting his hands up. Then he stepped in close and took Cass's wrists in his hands. "I want to help. You're . . . you're important."

Cass stared at Farryn, her cheeks burning, not knowing what to say, and then he started to blush, too. He let go of her wrists. "Besides," he said, with a forced grin. "What else am I going to do? Stay here and limp around, burning squirrel meat?"

"You can stay here and keep healing," Cass said. "And not get killed because I dragged you into my stupid plan."

"I'm fine," Farryn said. "Good as new with Kevin's leg. And I won't get killed."

"Okay," Cass heard herself say. She saw Farryn's face light up. She hugged him, and he hugged her back, hard. She was making a mistake, a selfish mistake, a small part of her knew. But mostly she was happy that she wouldn't be alone.

CHAPTER 20

TWO DAYS LATER, THE REBELS BROKE CAMP TO HEAD FOR THEIR NEW base. They headed south in tense silence, sticking to the trees as much as possible, but using roadways in brief bursts when it was impossible to avoid them.

Nick realized, as he walked, that he could tell which rebels had come from a City, and which had been from Freeposts, just by the way they walked. Everyone was fairly quiet, especially considering how much they were carrying, but some were a bit lighter on their feet and avoided making almost any sounds— the ones who had spent the most time as Freeposters. Others stepped on the occasional branch, dislodged the occasional rock down a hill—these, of course, were the rebels who had spent more time living in the Cities. He wondered how they had ended up with Clay's rebels. How had they escaped? They all had stories to tell, he was sure. But not many in that group were big talkers.

Kevin had gone a day ahead, which Nick wasn't thrilled about, but at least Cass and Farryn were hiking with the group, Farryn limping along on the prosthetic leg but somehow keeping pace. And Nick was quietly very happy that Lexi was walking alongside him. She wasn't talking to him, but she was apparently willing to be next to him, and Nick took that as a good sign.

After a day and a half of hard hiking, they hunkered down a half mile north of the City, behind a row of burned-out pre-Rev buildings along a cratered, warped roadway. The tall City buildings loomed in the distance, gray and white and black against the pale blue sky. Nobody spoke. A few rebels napped, their backs against the broken walls. Nick couldn't imagine how they were able to sleep; he was so full of nervous energy. He ate a biscuit from his pack, and checked and rechecked the burst rifle he had been issued.

"It's fine," Lexi said. "You're going to break it if you keep messing with it."

Nick looked up, startled; these were the first words Lexi had said to him in days. He repressed a smile, although he felt like grinning from ear to ear. He wasn't sure if it would make her mad.

"You're right," he said carefully. He tried to keep his tone neutral; he didn't want to scare Lexi away or say something that would cause her anger to rise up again. "Just nervous, I guess."

Lexi took a piece of Nick's biscuit and chewed it slowly, looking off to the south at the City. "Me, too," she said.

"You'll be okay," Nick said. "Ro won't have you in the front attack."

"I'm not worried about myself!" Lexi snapped.

Nick's heart sank. Had he screwed up again, so quickly?

But then Lexi's frown softened, and she even gave him a weak little smile. "You really are an idiot, aren't you? You've got no idea what to say or do."

Nick couldn't hold back his smile, realizing that Lexi was forgiving him.

Lexi's smile broadened, too, and she reached out and pushed a strand of Nick's hair back from his eyes. "You need a haircut," she said. "When this is over, I'm gonna chop you."

Nick still didn't trust himself to speak. He just kept smiling.

Lexi laughed. "Stop grinning, you idiot," she said.

"I'm sorry," he said, and forced his smile down.

"And no more apologizing. Just stop being such an idiot, okay, rock star?"

"Yeah, sure, whatever you say," Nick said. "Look, you know I don't care about Erica the way I care about you. . . ."

"Idiot!" Lexi said. "Shut up."

Nick shut his mouth and nodded.

"Better," Lexi said. She looked back at the City in the distance, and her expression grew anxious again. "I'm worried for you, and for everyone in the City. My friends. My parents." She looked back at Nick. "What's going to happen to them?"

Now Nick really did feel like a fool. Lexi had left her whole life behind in the City. She was so tough, so quick to adapt, so uncomplaining, that he hadn't given any thought to her parents, left behind in the City. "They'll be fine," Nick said. "We'll find your parents and we'll get them out."

"What if we can't find them, Nick? What if they get hurt?"

"We'll find them," repeated Nick, looking out at the City. But Lexi was right—the City was going to be chaos when they attacked. What if they couldn't find her parents, or *his* parents? Would he have to abandon them again? He sighed, and then thought about Kevin, and felt even more worried. Was his brother in the City now, invisible? He should have done more to stop Kevin.

Nick heard it first . . . the crackle of underbrush, possibly. He wasn't even sure what had triggered his wariness . . . and he was on his feet, rifle aimed back at the trees to the northeast. A moment later Ro was at his side, his hand on the barrel of Nick's rifle, pushing it down.

"Stand down, Nick," he said. "You got bot ears, too?"

Nick let his rifle drop.

A moment later the first rebel, a woman Nick had never seen before, appeared from the trees. She wore camouflage gear and had a pistol at her waist. A man followed close behind, then two more men, and then more. . . . Nick counted forty fighters, men and women, none of whom he had ever seen. They all quickly took cover behind the buildings, crouching down next to Ro's fighters. Clay, he realized, had called in more troops. Nick felt a new tingle of anticipation in his fingers and toes. This really was going to be a big battle.

Ro shook hands with the woman who had appeared first. "Helena?" he said.

"Yes," said the woman. "You are Ro?" Her voice was gravelly, and deep for a woman.

Ro nodded. "The groups to the south are in place?"

"Correct," she said. She scratched her cheek, then flicked dirt out of her fingernail. "So this new tech the General has— it really works?"

Ro shrugged and checked his comm bracelet. "We'll know soon enough."

CHAPTER 21

KEVIN LAY IN A DITCH, UNDER TREE COVER, JUST A FEW HUNDRED yards outside the City. It may even have been the same ditch that he and Nick and Cass had lain in, what seemed like a lifetime ago, when they were first scouting the City—it certainly had a similar view. Next to him rested the Wall unit, humming gently, and between the unit and the road crouched Wynn. Apparently, Kevin thought, looking at the scar on her cheek while she stared at the nearby City, she was his go-to babysitter.

It had been twenty minutes since Grennel, three other men, and two women, all laden down with as much weaponry and explosives as they could carry, had donned their vests and disappeared when Kevin triggered the Wall unit. The

City remained quiet and calm, and the anticipation was killing Kevin. Even Wynn seemed agitated, shifting her weight quietly back and forth from foot to foot, tapping silently but steadily on the barrel of her rifle with her left forefinger.

And then, finally, the first explosion came, louder than Kevin had imagined it would be. The ground beneath him vibrated. Another explosion followed, and another. Those would be the first strikes on the central administration and communication centers.

"Here we go," whispered Wynn, gripping her burst rifle, her eyes locked on the City. Kevin quickly slipped on the extra vest he had hidden in the bottom of his pack and flicked the dampening clamp from full block to thirty percent.

It seemed to be working, according to the readouts, but he wasn't sure until Wynn glanced back, then jumped to her feet, a look of alarm on her face. "What the hell?" she said. "Kevin!"

Kevin quickly ran past Wynn, careful not to make any sound, then jogged up the road and into the City, grinning like an idiot.

On the outskirts of the City people were milling about, on the sidewalks, in the streets next to their abandoned scoots, confused and nervous, looking into the center of the City. Kevin carefully made his way around them, unnoticed, and it was the strangest feeling—both exhilarating, like he was an invisible superhero, and unnerving, like he was dead, a ghost.

And then there was another explosion, this one much louder, just a few blocks away. It knocked Kevin back a step. A ball of fire rose into the air, and a five-story building collapsed with a rumbling roar. Up the road a Petey hurried past. Lase bursts flared with their crackling hums.

A woman near Kevin screamed, and suddenly everyone on the street was running, scattering in different directions, scrambling for shelter. A man slammed into Kevin, sending Kevin crashing painfully onto the street. The man stopped and looked around wildly for a moment, then kept running. Kevin got up as quickly as he could, and hurried over to crouch next to an overturned scoot. His shoulder was bruised, but he was otherwise unhurt. He nervously checked the vest. The wiring seemed intact, and the clamp seemed to be working fine—still receiving energy, still dampening it to thirty percent.

The exhilaration was now gone, replaced by something that Kevin had to admit felt a lot like fear. He waited a moment, steadying himself. Nick, of course, rust him, had been right: This was a war zone. He needed to pay attention, or, invisible or not, he was going to get himself killed.

A sphere bot shot past, and then another, and Kevin instinctively ducked for cover before forcing himself to stand up. "Come on, idiot," he whispered. "Let's get this over with."

As he made his way carefully across the City toward his parents' neighborhood, he saw fewer people outside—they had all taken shelter where they could. The explosions continued, as well as the lase blasts, but whenever he saw a flash he moved in a different direction. He didn't want to catch any crossfire. From what he saw of the bots, before quickly ducking away, they were being decimated—they were firing shots wildly, indiscriminately, while the shots aimed at them were deadly accurate. The cloaking devices were obviously working fine for the others as well.

More and more buildings were burning and shattered as he crossed the City, and Kevin began seeing human bodies crushed and burned, lying in the rubble. It was the Island all over again, on a larger scale. He hurried forward as quickly as he could, trying not to look at the dead.

He paused to get his bearings, and he realized that he was near the re-education center, which was good, very good. . . . His parents were nearby. If, of course, they were in the same apartment. He didn't let himself linger on that thought. They had to be there. He had built a rusted *invisibility suit* so he could come and get them.

The door of the building in front of him exploded outward, the windows of the first floor shattering in a rain of glass, and Kevin was flung to the street by the blast. He landed hard on his stomach, awkwardly twisting to try to block his fall with his hands. He lay on the ground for a moment, stunned. *Did the blast come from inside the building?* he wondered, trying to pull his scattered thoughts together. He pushed himself to his feet and looked down, and his heart froze.

The dampening clamp was cracked and hung off his vest by two loose, frayed wires.

"Rust!" he said. "Rust, rust, rust!" He checked the readouts, which were of course dead.

The vest began to feel warm, and for a moment Kevin thought he was just imagining it, but then the warmth intensified, becoming a burning heat, and Kevin tore the vest off his body. It was beginning to glow and smoke; it burned his hand, so he dropped it to the ground. He bent down, to try to disengage the faulty clamp—it was obviously drawing in a full load of energy, overloading the vest circuit. He touched the clamp, to turn it toward him, and it burned his fingers. "Damn!" he said, shaking his hand, sticking his fingers in his mouth. The vest's glow intensified, and Kevin took a step back, and then the vest began to emit a high-pitched whine and the glow became painfully bright.

"Crap," Kevin whispered. He scrambled backward, tripping over the street curb, landing on his butt, and then he ducked his head as the vest flared even brighter and burst into flames.

Kevin lay on the ground, watching the vest burn, black smoke rising up into the sky. He was in the middle of the City. Alone. During a battle.

Completely, starkly, utterly visible.

Kevin heard the rumbling of a Petey up ahead, to the left, and he scrambled to his feet and began to run. He ducked to the right and ran hard, down the street that led toward the re-education center. He wildly tried to formulate a new plan—should he find somewhere to hide until Clay's main forces took control? Try to get back out of the City? Should he just move forward with his original plan, broken camo vest be damned, and find his parents?

He glanced back over his shoulder and saw the Petey raising its lase arm, and he tried for an extra burst of speed, to make the next intersection so he could cut away. His legs and lungs were aching. Then the pavement below his feet was lifting, separating into chunks, and there was a roar in his ears, and he pinwheeled his arms and legs as he flew. He landed hard on his left side. His head slapped against the ground, and he plunged into blackness.

CHAPTER 22

THERE WAS AN ORANGE FLASH, NEAR THE CENTER OF THE CITY, FOL-
lowed a moment later by a rumbling roar that pushed Nick and
Lexi backward a step. The rest of the rebels were quickly on
their feet, guns at the ready, staring at the City. Another explosion hit, and then another. Smoke began to rise. Nick thought
he could see lase flashes among the buildings. He strained to
see, and then his bot eye suddenly engaged. His vision tun-
neled and zoomed, and he could clearly see Hightown, two
buildings reduced to rubble, a third in flames, and lase bursts
flickering through the streets. Instinctively he started to move
toward the City; Lexi and others around him were doing the
same.

"Hold your positions!" shouted Ro.

"Nobody moves until given the order!" added Helena.

Nick froze, and returned to his position behind a dirt mound. Another explosion rocked the ground, and then a third. He gritted his teeth and gripped his blast rifle hard. Lexi sat close to him, their shoulders touching. They waited. Five minutes passed. There were more explosions, more lase bursts. A fire began spreading through Hightown. Ten minutes went by, agony for Nick. He wanted to be in there, killing bots, finding his parents, somehow keeping Kevin from doing something stupid. . . . He couldn't stand any more waiting.

He was so intent on watching the City that he didn't notice Cass until she was at his side, hugging him. He started, tensed, and then relaxed when he saw who it was.

"Be careful," Cass said.

"I will," Nick said. He hesitated. "I'll try to find your birth parents," he said. There was another rumbling explosion, a big one that Nick could feel in his feet, and he quickly looked at the City, then back to Cass.

"You don't even know what they look like, or where they live, you idiot," she said. She smiled. "But thank you."

"Why are all the girls in my life constantly calling me an idiot?" Nick said.

Cass and Lexi laughed. "Because you are," Cass said.

Farryn limped up to Nick and shook his hand. "Good luck," he said.

"Watch out for my sister while I'm gone," Nick said.

"I promise," said Farryn solemnly.

Nick nodded. He was grateful that Cass had Farryn; he knew that Farryn would do everything he could to protect his sister. "Stay safe," he said to Cass, giving her another quick hug. "I'll see you when I get back."

Nick was about to turn back to the City, but Cass had a strange look on her face that caught his eye. It was almost a look of guilt. . . . "What is it, Cass?" he said.

Cass hesitated, looking away from him, biting her lip, shaking her head, then she took a deep breath and turned back to him, and Nick felt a sense of dread even before she opened her mouth. "Nick," Cass said quietly. "I'm getting my family out. My birth parents, and my sister."

"What?" Nick said. "That's crazy. . . . You've got to stay back, with Farryn. . . ."

"Look, Nick," Cass began, but stopped when Ro approached.

"It's time," Ro said. "Nick and Lexi, you're with me. Cass, Farryn, you're hanging back in reserve."

Ro began to walk away.

"Cass," said Nick, "you've got to stay back. Please."

"Nick!" said Ro, glancing back. "I said *with me*! Now!"

"Don't worry about me," Cass said.

Nick knew his sister, and he knew that look of determination on her face. He groaned with frustration and anger and worry. He had to go . . . but he couldn't leave his sister, just to let her sneak into the City and get killed. "Damn it, Cass."

"Nick!" shouted Ro.

Nick gave Cass a quick hug and grabbed her shoulders hard. "Don't," he said, looking her in the eyes. "Please." Cass shrugged out of his grip, and didn't say anything.

"Nick, Lexi, *now*!" said Ro.

Nick let go of Cass, and he and Lexi hurried after Ro. Tears threatened to well up in Nick's human eye. First his brother, now his sister . . . *Were they going to end up scattered again? Dead?* If anything happened to either one of them . . . he could barely handle even the thought. He'd never forgive himself.

Ro gathered his forces into two groups of fifteen. "This is hopefully a mop-up," Ro said. "Our advance team has knocked out key comm sites and defenses, but there will be bots remaining. We go in, we find all the bots we can, we kill them, and we evacuate the survivors who can move quickly. We need to be gone before the bots from another City figure out what's going on and scramble air defenses. One hour. Understood?" Everyone nodded. "Comm check." He tapped his wrist comm. Nick's comm flickered at his wrist. He tapped it, sending a clear signal to Ro. He took one last look into the camp, looking for Cass, but he couldn't see her.

Ro smiled grimly. "Let's go take this rusted City back."

CHAPTER 23

ONCE THE EXPLOSIONS BEGAN, IT WAS EASY FOR CASS AND FARRYN TO slip away with backpacks, a few packets of energy paste, a hunting knife, and a lase pistol. Cass carried the gun; she was the better shot.

They made their way carefully toward the City, ducking the sparks from the disabled power grid. Cass had to slow her pace for Farryn. She felt selfish for agreeing to let him come, and fearful, because his awkwardness might get them both killed. She pushed the thoughts aside. It was too late now. What was it her mom used to say? "You made your bed—you lie in it."

The City streets, at the edge of the town, were empty. Everyone seemed to be taking shelter. Cass found an abandoned scoot that had been left on its side in the street. Farryn climbed on behind her, and they began heading for Hightown. The street was still devoid of people, and bots. She leaned forward and increased her speed. *Is it really going to be this easy?* she let herself wonder.

There was a crackle of lase fire a block ahead of her, and then an explosion, followed by a shower of glass, and the road buckled, sending Cass and Farryn flying over the handlebars.

Cass ducked and rolled, landing hard against the curb, and the breath was knocked out of her. When she could breathe again she did a quick scan of her body—some scrapes, but nothing broken or cut too badly—and then she hurried over to Farryn, who had come to rest a few feet away from her.

He was slowly getting to his feet, groaning.

"Are you okay?" she said. Sarah's lessons on first aid rushed through her head—how to apply a tourniquet to stop bleeding, immobilize breaks and fractures, gauge the probability of concussion.

Farryn began patting his body, starting at his shoulders, working down to his legs, and when he touched his right calf, he gave an exaggerated look of panic and said, "My leg! I can't feel my leg!"

Cass punched him on the shoulder, hard. "Hilarious," she said, suppressing a laugh.

Farryn grinned, rubbing his shoulder.

There was another burst of lase fire, farther away, but still close, and Farryn and Cass ducked for cover into an alleyway.

They waited, watching the street ahead of them. Cass gripped her pistol hard, and Farryn held his knife ready. *What are we doing?* she thought. *How in the world are we going to fight a City full of bots with a lase pistol and a hunting knife?* She almost laughed—it was ridiculous.

The street remained clear. Cass was about to step out, when a Petey and a sphere bot appeared in the intersection ahead. Farryn grabbed her shoulder and yanked her hard against the alley wall.

"I see them!" she hissed.

"Sorry," whispered Farryn.

The Petey raised its arm, and began firing its lase down the connecting street, at something Cass couldn't see. There was a burst of return fire that missed the Petey and crashed into a nearby storefront, shattering the glass. The sphere bot bobbed, and with a burst of sudden speed began coming down the street toward their hiding spot. The Petey ducked, continuing to fire its lase, and then a burst hit it, and another, and a third, knocking the bot back, and the Petey's lase arm flailed wildly, releasing a burst that struck the wall fifteen feet above Cass's and Farryn's heads and showered them with chips of concrete and glass. They both hunkered down instinctively, Farryn wrapping his arms around Cass and covering her with his body.

Cass quickly shrugged Farryn off, looking for the sphere bot—there, it was still coming toward them; it would see them soon. Cass thumbed her pistol to full burst, praying that it would be enough to take down the sphere. She aimed, trying to track the bot's flight, held her breath, and squeezed the trigger. The burst hit the sphere with a crackling thump and the bot dropped to the ground like a stone, cracked open and smoking.

After that they stayed on foot, moving in quick bursts of speed—as best as Farryn was able—from cover to cover. They saw three Peteys destroyed, and four sphere bots. Cass took down another sphere on her own.

As they drew closer to Hightown—the center of the bot control, where Cass knew the rebels had focused their initial surprise attacks—the damage to the City grew more devastating. Entire buildings were reduced to pieces, aflame. Burned and broken human bodies were scattered among the rubble. *How many people are buried inside each collapsed building?* Cass thought angrily. *Hundreds? Thousands? Are my parents among the dead? My sister? My birth parents? Lexi's parents? Farryn's father?* She forced the thought back. *Stay alive*, she told herself. *Keep Farryn alive. Get to Hightown. Find your birth parents and Penny. Nick will get Mom and Dad.*

They neared the Hightown block that Cass remembered— Cass hoped her fuzzy memory wasn't letting her down—and she held her breath as they turned the corner. She let her breath out. There was the high-rise, still standing. Two other structures on the street were crumbled, but her birth parents' building stood tall and untouched.

She was about to run for the entrance, but Farryn grabbed her shoulder and pulled her back against a wall. A group of rebels entered the street from the north, walking quickly, fanned out to cover all angles of attack. Cass recognized some of them from the camp, and then she saw Nick, in the front next to Ro, and she felt a dizzy rush—he had blood on his cheek but he was okay, he seemed okay—and she wanted to call out to him, but she kept her mouth shut and crouched down deeper into the shadow of the wall. Ro would not be happy to see her and Farryn in the City. She quietly watched her brother walk away, his face lit by the flickering fires of the burning City, and she felt like crying.

Farryn put his hand on her shoulder and squeezed. "He'll be fine," he whispered.

Cass put her hand on top of Farryn's, and nodded, not trusting herself to speak.

Nick and Ro and the other rebels turned the corner, and Cass stood, making a dash for the building. The front door was unlocked—the locks must not work with the power grid out, she realized—and she entered the dark foyer, Farryn behind her. Cass reached for the elevator controls, then stopped herself. *Foolish. Elevator isn't going to work without power.* "Come on," she said. "The stairs."

Cass took the stairs two at a time, feeling the adrenaline rush of being so close. After a few flights she glanced back, and slowed herself down. Farryn was laboring to keep up, his prosthetic awkward on the steps. His face was pale and streaked with sweat.

He shouldn't be here, Cass thought. *I shouldn't have let him come. He just lost his leg last week.* Cass waited for him to catch up. "Farryn—" she began, but he cut her off.

"I'm fine," he said angrily. "I'll keep up. Go."

She resumed climbing, but set a slower pace, Farryn breathing hard behind her. Finally they reached the twelfth floor. The hallway was dim; only the emergency lightstrips were working. Cass knocked hard on the first doorway. She thought this was the right one, but she wasn't entirely sure. It might have been the next one. . . .

"Mother!" she yelled. "Father!" It felt artificial, forced, to be calling them that, but it was what they would recognize. "Penny!" There was no answer. She pounded harder and kicked, but there was still no response, so she moved to the next door, hoping that she had been confused. She couldn't imagine coming all this way, risking all this, dragging Farryn into this, all for nothing. . . .

She began pounding and calling on the second door, and it was flung open, and Penny stood there. "Cass!" she screamed, and flung herself into Cass's arms. Cass hugged her tightly, and all her doubt vanished. Her sister needed her. Cass had come to save her. She could smell her little sister's shampoo, a flowery soapy scent that was unlike anything from out in the woods.

"I'm back," she said, pressing her nose into the top of her little sister's head and breathing in.

"Cass!" her mother said. "It's really you!" She rushed forward and joined in the hug, crushing Penny between them. After a long moment she let go and stepped back, keeping her hands on Cass's shoulders. "What happened to you?" she said. "Are you okay? You have to come in. . . . There's something terrible happening outside, we have to stay inside, where it's safe. . . ."

"No," Cass said. "We have to go. It's not safe here."

"We can't leave now," said Cass's father, who stood in the background, near the entrance to the kitchen. Cass hadn't even seen him there, in the dim emergency lighting, until he had spoken. "There's something happening, some sort of power grid failure, explosions. . . . We need to stay inside, and stay out of the robots' way so they can get it under control."

"It's an attack," Cass said. "The rebels . . ." she began, then stopped. There was so much her parents didn't understand. She tried again. "A group of humans from the woods is attacking. They're destroying the bots. They're taking the City back."

Her mother went pale, and dropped her hands to her sides, and her father shook his head. "No, that can't be," he said. "The City can't exist without the robots. You must be confused. . . ."

"There's no time for this!" Cass snapped. "Look out the window! The City is under attack, and half of Hightown is burning, and this building could be next! We have to get out of here, now!"

It was Penny who crossed over to the window. "Window, clear," she said. Nothing happened. She looked back at her parents, confused, and her father walked over to a control box in the living room and played with the settings. The emergency lights dimmed even more, leaving them in murky near-darkness. "Try it now," he said.

"Window, clear," Penny repeated, and the window slowly clarified from opaque to transparent. She looked out, and her father crossed the room to join her. Cass's mother stayed back, away from the window, one hand over her mouth, the other hugging her waist.

Penny began to shake and cry. "It's all burning," she said. Her father hugged her.

"Cass," Farryn said, "we need to go."

Cass stepped into the room. "If you want to stay alive, we need to go now," she said firmly. Her father looked at her, a blank, lost expression on his face, and then he slowly nodded.

CHAPTER 24

THE PETEY STAGGERED BACKWARD INTO A DOORWAY WHEN NICK'S BLAST hit it in the chest. The door crumpled inward, shattered by the immense weight of the bot. It took the Petey a few moments to clear itself of the rubble, firing its lase arms wildly in an effort to protect itself. Another rifle blast hit it, from the fighter to Nick's left, and another, and then a third, this one from Lexi. The Petey's armor cracked, exposing a tangle of wiring, and it ground to a halt, its arms suddenly hanging limp.

"Nick, clean it up," said Ro. Nick thumbed his rifle to low burst—no need to drain the battery with anything larger when the armor was cracked—and squeezed off the shot. The burst hit the crippled Petey right in the large gap on its chest, and the bot shattered. Neo-plas and metal alloy flew thirty feet in every direction, and the rebels ducked for cover. Ro laughed and clapped Nick on the back.

There was a flash of light and the sidewalk at their feet exploded, sending up a shower of concrete and dirt and knocking Ro and Nick to the ground.

"Petey, ten o'clock!" a nearby fighter shouted, releasing a burst from his rifle. Nick, dazed, staggered to his feet. Lexi grabbed his forearm to steady him. *Damn it*, he thought. *Where did that Petey come from?* Another blast from the bot crackled past his left shoulder, and the man next to him screamed and went down. Three bursts from the rebels hit the bot, and it fell backward. Lexi's hand dug painfully into Nick's arm. She pulled him to cover, but through the smoke of the explosion, Nick saw that Ro was down.

"Go!" he yelled at Lexi. With a look that said she wasn't going anywhere, she began climbing over rubble and helped Nick heave Ro to his feet. Ro had blood on his forehead, and his eyes were glassy and dazed. Nick hooked one of Ro's arms over his shoulder, Lexi the other, and together they dragged Ro toward cover. They managed a crouching, staggering run toward the corner of a building. After a few seconds Ro began to revive, and by the time they neared the wall, where the rest of the group had already hidden, Ro was bearing his own weight.

"I'm fine," he said, leaning against the wall, wiping the blood away from his eye. He nodded at Nick and Lexi. "Thank you," he said.

"I didn't see that one," said Nick. "Wasn't paying attention—" His bot eye caught a flicker of movement up and to the right, and he wheeled, sighted the sphere bot, and aimed. But before he could squeeze off a shot another burst hit it, sending the bot to the ground.

The burst had come from the other side of the street—which was empty. *What the hell?* Nick thought.

He heard footsteps running on the street, approaching, and his bot eye scanned frantically. Nothing. But he could hear footsteps, and then he heard a quiet, low laugh. Suddenly a man appeared from nowhere.

Nick let out a strangled yell, then realized he recognized the figure. It was Parson, one of Clay's rebels, wearing one of Kevin's camouflage suits. He took his hand off the control knob on his vest, and nodded at Nick, grinning. "Didn't mean to scare ya," he said.

"Didn't," Nick said.

Parson turned to Ro. "Scout bots still giving away your positions?" he said.

Ro nodded.

"We're still working on getting all the General's comm targets. Just be careful, and keep an eye out for the spheres."

"Just get the damned comm targets down," said Ro. He tore a strip of cloth off the bottom of his shirt, and tied it around his forehead to cover the gash that was still oozing blood into his eyes.

Parson twisted the controls on his vest, and disappeared.

Nick could hear him jogging away. The hairs on the back of his neck prickled.

Ro's team slowly worked their way farther into the City, where they were to rendezvous in Hightown with the other teams pushing in from the perimeter. Fighting inward from all directions, by the time the rebels reached Hightown, the City would be under their control.

They took down four more Peteys and five spheres, and lost one more rebel, a woman who had her neck broken by a falling chunk of wall. Ro took her rifle, closed her eyes with his fingertips, then grimly moved on, leaving her under the rubble.

As they approached Hightown, the bot engagements became less frequent—maybe the camouflaged fighters were thinning them out, Nick guessed—but they came across more and more City residents out on the streets.

Their homes had been destroyed, and they had nowhere to go. Some huddled amid the rubble, weeping, trying desperately to find cover. Others were too dazed and shocked to function—Nick passed by men and women who were just sitting on the street corners, their faces blank, their clothes torn and bloody. Most didn't even look up as Nick passed them. One man shuffled past, moaning, his feet bare and bloody, his face scorched red and blistered. Others lay dead on the street, crushed by the collapsed buildings, burned by the explosions, lased by crossfire.

Nick held down the nausea and horror that threatened to overcome him as he searched the faces for anyone he might recognize—his parents, most of all, but also Kevin and Cass and Farryn, as well as Doc, and Lexi's parents. Nobody, alive or dead, looked familiar.

Ro called out to the survivors as they passed. "Come with us! We're here to free you from the bots! Come with us and fight!" A very few joined them—four men and two women. Ro quietly signaled for two of the rebels to loop back to the rear, to keep the survivors under watch.

Most of the people on the streets ignored Ro, or went scrambling for cover when they saw the rebels approaching and refused to come out. "Idiots," he muttered quietly to himself, but loud enough for Nick, standing next to him, to hear. "We're offering them freedom."

Nick stepped around the body of a man lying on the street corner, arms bent at unnatural angles under his torso. He forced himself to study the face—no, nobody he knew—and then he looked away, fighting back the urge to throw up. *Yeah*, he thought bitterly. *Freedom.*

And then he looked back at the body, suddenly realizing— yes, the man was wearing a tan jumpsuit. He looked around the street. Of course. He had been so preoccupied with the hunt for bots, with the pitiful survivors, the dead, that he hadn't even realized that he was a half block from the re-education center.

There it was, on the left. It was on fire, flames licking out the shattered windows. The roof of the building had collapsed, pancaking the floor below it, and the rest of the structure was threatening to collapse as well.

Nick froze in his tracks, staring, remembering. He hoped every last one of the rusted Lecturer bots was in there, destroyed. But how many people were inside? How many men and women and kids in jumpsuits lay on the white tiles, overcome by smoke, crushed by the collapsed building, burned? He wanted to rush into the building and look for survivors, but he forced himself to turn away. There was no time. And all he'd manage to do would be to get himself killed.

If he was near the re-education center, he knew, then that meant he was only a few blocks away from his parents' apartment. He looked off to the west, where flames and smoke rose up into the sky. *No* . . . He felt a dizzy rush of panic. *They have to be okay.* . . .

"Lexi, I'll be back," he said.

"Where are you going?" Lexi said.

"Gotta check out my parents' neighborhood. We're close."

"I'll go with you," Lexi said.

"No!" he said harshly, and then, more softly, "Please. Stay with the team. It's safer."

"No deal," said Lexi. "I'm going with you."

Nick hesitated, then realized there was no way Lexi was going to back down, so he just nodded.

"Ro," Nick said, fighting to keep his voice calm. "Lexi and I need to go check something out. We'll find you at the rendezvous."

Ro shook his head. "No. We stick together."

Nick gritted his teeth, rushed through the options. He had to go, there was no question of that. . . . Should he just take off running? Ro wouldn't shoot him in the back, would he? Or he could come up with some sort of plausible lie . . . or . . . "My parents," Nick said, desperate enough to just try the truth. "We're near where they must be. There's fire . . . I need to get them out."

Ro stared at Nick. Nick gripped his gun tightly, waiting, forcing himself to wait, to not just say to hell with Ro and take off.

Ro nodded. "Be quick," he said. "Don't waste any time."

Nick felt like he had been released out of a starting gate. He nodded at Lexi and took off running, west, along a side street. Lexi followed close behind. He kept an eye out for bots, his hand near the trigger of his rifle—he wouldn't be much help to his parents if he got himself killed. And he couldn't let Lexi get hurt. He darted past abandoned scoots and around bombed-out rubble, giving a wide berth to a storefront that was on fire, the flames flaring out the broken window.

He ran four blocks west, one block north, his heart in his throat. He could hear the crackling roar of the fire ahead. The air was smoky and he could feel the rising heat on his cheeks.

His parents were so close . . . they had to be okay . . . he'd find them . . . they'd be so relieved . . . he'd bring them to the rendezvous and then out of the City and the medic would remove his mother's chip and then they'd finally, finally be a family again. . . .

Nick turned the corner and stumbled to a halt. His parents' entire block was aflame, fire raging through the rubble. Not one building had been left standing. The first thing his scrambled brain recognized was the heat, the intense heat on his face.

"Which one is it?" said Lexi.

Nick didn't answer. He didn't even know which building was his parents'. It didn't matter—nobody could be alive in any of the buildings. He took a stumbling step forward, into the street lined on both sides by collapsed, burning devastation.

"Mom!" he yelled. "Dad!" He walked down the middle of the street. He was crying, but the heat evaporated the tears on his face.

"Mom!"

Nothing moved except for the fire. There was no sound except for the roar of the flickering flames. He sat down in the middle of the street, rifle across his legs. He stopped crying; now he just felt numb. His parents, if they were in their home, were dead. All he could do was hope they had gotten out, that they were alive somewhere in the City. But no, they were probably dead, their bodies just feet away. Crushed. Burned.

A whir of motion in the air to his left caught Nick's attention, and his bot eye zoomed and targeted, and before he could even think, he was on his feet, releasing a blast at the sphere bot that had appeared over the wreckage forty feet away. His blast hit the bot squarely, and it burst open with a loud pop and a flare of green-tinged flames, and crashed to the ground.

"Goddamned rusted bots!" he yelled. He shot another burst into the broken husk of the sphere, sending the bot flying up and backward. He watched it roll to a stop, separating into two pieces like a cracked egg.

"Nick!" said Lexi. "Let's move! They're not here. They must have evacuated."

"Damned bots," he said again, quietly. "And damned Clay."

"Come on," Lexi said. "They're not here! I need to see about my parents, too."

Nick looked up at her, feeling a rush of shame. Of course . . . Lexi's parents . . . Hopefully one good thing could come out of this rusted mission.

They found two scoots, but Lexi had him climb on the back of hers. "I remember how you drive," she said. Nick didn't argue; she was right. It would be ridiculous, after all he'd been through, to get himself killed by falling off a scoot.

They rode as quickly as possible, picking through the obstacles—the overturned scoots, the broken, smoking shells of bots, the collapsed buildings, the dead bodies. Nick forced himself to check every one. He recognized none of them.

Two were so badly burned that he couldn't make out their features, but they were both very tall, much taller than his parents, or Cass, or Kevin. The streets, as they drove away from Hightown, were empty of people—living people, at least—but Nick could see the occasional face in a dimly lit window, peering out at them as they rode past. How long were they going to hide in their homes, in the sacked City, waiting for their lives to return to normal? Would they ever come out?

Nick felt Lexi's body tense as they approached her block, then relax when they turned onto her street and saw that her neighborhood was untouched. He couldn't believe, despite everything, that he could be distracted by the way her back felt, leaning against his chest, and her waist in his hands, but he was.

The front door to Lexi's house was wide open. Lexi jumped off her scoot and rushed inside, leaving Nick to figure out how to park the scoot. He quickly gave up, let the scoot topple onto its side, and hurried after her.

They searched every room, Lexi calling out for her parents, but the house was empty. Lexi stood in the living room, her hands on her hips, saying nothing and staring at the entrance to the kitchen.

"We need to go, Lexi," Nick said. "They must be okay. You saw how they had gone through their clothes, and the kitchen cabinets are open. . . . It looks like they packed up and got out of here in a hurry."

Lexi's shoulders began to gently shake, and she lowered her head to her chest and wrapped her arms tightly around herself. It took a moment for Nick to realize that she was crying. He was stunned—Lexi was too tough, too strong to cry—but then he pulled her into a big hug. She resisted, then turned and put her face in his chest and began sobbing.

He held her tight, not knowing what to say, or what else to do. He felt useless. Soon Lexi calmed down, and pushed him away, stepping back. She wiped the tears off her face with the back of her hand.

"I miss them, Nick," she said. "I left them and they don't even know if I'm alive and I feel horrible." She looked like she was going to start crying again, and Nick stepped toward her, but she held her hands up, clenched her jaw, and with a visible effort of will, kept control. "Rust!" she said. "Enough of this stupid weeping. Come on. We need to get back to Ro."

She pushed past Nick and out the door. Nick watched her walk away, still feeling as if he should have said something, or done something, more.

They ditched the scoot near the center of Hightown. Two rebels stood on the street corner, their backs to the center of town, guns at the ready. Nick was careful to make his and Lexi's presence known right away with a whistle. The guards swung their guns toward him. "We're with Clay!" he called out. "Ro's team."

The guards nodded, and waved him past with the muzzles of their guns, then returned to their scan of the street. *Security perimeter*, Nick realized, looking down a street to his left, seeing another pair of rebel guards at the far intersection.

In the center of Hightown, Nick found that a hundred rebels had gathered, along with an equal number of survivors. The City survivors looked haggard and nervous. Most were empty-handed, but some carried a few random supplies—packages of dehydrated food, extra clothes. One woman, her face pale, her eyes wide and unblinking, held a shivering black poodle.

Nick pushed through the crowd, looking for his parents, and Lexi's parents, and Kevin, and Cass, and Farryn. He recognized nobody. He kept shoving through the people, standing on tiptoes, trying to cover the entire crowd. Nick grew more desperate as he worked his way through the group, and his eyes began to sting, threatening tears again, but he held back the panic and the tears. He was not going to be weak in front of all these people.

He circled through the entire crowd, searching, and came back to his starting point. Nobody he knew. Should he go back out into the City to search? Where would he even begin? He didn't know what to do.

He began to edge to the perimeter of the crowd—maybe he'd just pick a direction, and start looking—and then he saw Clay enter from a side street and climb onto a pile of rubble. She raised her arms, and the crowd, with prompting from the rebels, quieted. General Clay raised her long arms above her head and gave a victory yell.

"This has been a glorious first strike," she shouted out to the crowd, "but it is only the beginning. For those of you who have elected to join us, I applaud you for taking back your humanity." Clay paused, looking left and right, surveying the crowd. "We will be back, to gather more supplies. But for now, we need to return to the forest."

Nick thought she was done, but then she added, "And for those True Believers who refuse to accept their freedom, their humanity, who refuse to fight with us . . . they'll rust in hell along with the damned bots."

CHAPTER 25

WHEN FARRYN AND CASS AND HER FAMILY MADE IT OUT ONTO THE street, City 73 was strangely quiet. The fires still burned, but there was no lase fire, no explosions. Her parents and Penny just stood there, shrinking against the doorway, staring in stunned disbelief at the ruins of Hightown.

"It's going to be okay," said Cass's mother, pulling Penny close to her. "The robots will fix everything."

And that's when Cass realized she couldn't bring her family to Clay's camp. They were True Believers to the core. Her parents were thoroughly brainwashed, and her sister had never known anything other than the City. Clay would . . . Cass hesitated, hating to even think it, but she knew it was true. . . . Clay would have them killed.

So what to do? Where to take them? *Rust*, she thought, *I didn't plan this out very well.* "Come on," she said. "We've got to get out of the City." *I'll find a Freepost*, she decided. *Get them settled and safe.*

She realized this meant abandoning her brothers, but she had no choice. Her birth family wouldn't survive in the woods without her. She'd get back to her brothers when she could.

"We'll swing past your house on the way out," Cass said to Farryn. "See if your father is there."

Farryn nodded. He still looked pale, and his eyes were sunken. They began walking, and Cass noticed that his limp was more pronounced. This had been too much for him, she knew. She felt terribly guilty, but she was also immensely grateful. . . . She was parting with her brothers, for now, but at least she had Farryn with her.

Cass decided to risk scoots, since the fighting seemed to be over. They found three—Cass and Farryn on one, her parents on another, Penny on a third—and headed away from Hightown, toward Farryn's house.

It was slow going, having to pick their way through the rubble-strewn, chewed-up streets, but it was faster than walking, and Cass knew that Farryn needed the break. And as they moved farther from the center of the City, where the fighting had been less intense, they made better time.

They were only a few blocks from Farryn's house when Penny hit a pothole and tumbled off her bike. She landed on her left side and tucked into a roll, slamming her back hard against the curb.

Cass skidded to a halt, vaulted off her scoot, and ran to Penny, who was groaning, and pushing herself up onto her hands and knees.

"Penny!" Cass said, bending down and grabbing Penny's shoulders. "Are you okay?"

"I think so. . . ." Penny said. She had a cut on her cheek, and Penny touched it, then looked at the blood on her fingertips. "Oh my god," she said, panic in her voice. "I'm bleeding. . . ."

"You're okay," Cass said, cupping Penny's chin, turning her face to look at the cut. It was a long scratch along her jawline, but it didn't seem deep. *Facial cuts bleed profusely*, Sarah had taught Cass. *They often look worse than they really are.*

Her parents and Farryn were at her side. Her mother crushed Penny in a tight hug. "Penny! Are you okay? Your face . . ."

"Can you stand?" Cass said. "Does anything else hurt?"

Their mother helped Penny to her feet.

"My arm," Penny said, holding up her left forearm. It was badly scraped, with a gash near the elbow that was dripping blood. "Oh, no . . ."

"We need to get her to a rejuve tank!" said their mother.

Cass felt a flash of anger. There was no time for stupidity. "Let me see," she said, taking Penny's wrist. The cut thankfully had missed any major arteries and veins. It was jagged and dirty, but not too deep.

"It's okay," Cass said. She looked around, still holding Penny's wrist. "I need water and a bandage."

Farryn handed Cass a canteen, then tore off a strip from the bottom of his shirt. "I've always wanted to do that," he said, grinning.

Cass took the strip, shaking her head at Farryn, amused but not wanting to show it. She squirted water over the wound. Penny winced and reflexively tried to pull her arm away, but Cass held her tight. She took another look at the cut—the dirt was off, at least—and then she tied the strip of Farryn's shirt tight over Penny's forearm. "We'll clean that out better as soon as we have the chance. This'll stop the bleeding."

They reached Farryn's house without further incident, Penny switching with Farryn to ride behind Cass. The buildings on the block were all intact, except for a few broken windows. A scout bot lay in the middle of the road, scorched and crushed, a wisp of smoke still rising from it. Across the street a man and woman sat on their sidewalk. The man had his head in his hands, and the woman had her knees drawn up to her chest. Neither one said a word, or even looked at them when they pulled up on their scoots.

"Wait here," Cass said to her family, leaving them on Farryn's driveway. Penny stared into the street, at the broken bot, and hugged her mother's side. Her father ran his hands through his thin hair, and looked off in the distance toward Hightown, as if trying to decide whether he should go back.

The door vid plate wasn't working, so Farryn knocked hard on the door, then began kicking it. "Dad!" he yelled. There was no answer. He tried the door, and it swung open.

"Should have tried that first," he said, smiling. But Cass could tell he was nervous; his grin looked forced, like he was trying not to be sick. They entered the house, which was lit in the same murky emergency light as the Hightown apartment. "Dad!" Farryn called, but still got no answer.

They walked into the living room, kicking aside clothing, and dishes, and food packages strewn about the floor, and in the gloom they saw Farryn's father lying on the couch. He had one leg on the floor. One hand was on his belly, and the other was flung over his head. A large bottle, half-full of a brown liquid, lay on the ground next to him.

"Who's that?" he said, slurring his words.

"Dad, it's me. Farryn. We've gotta go."

"Farryn!" His father made a weak effort to sit up, then fell back on the couch. "You're gone. You went away."

"I'm back now," Farryn said. "I came back to get you. We have to go. We have to get out of the City."

His father didn't say anything, and Cass wondered if he had fallen asleep, or passed out, but then finally he said quietly, "No."

"Dad—" began Farryn.

"No!" his father yelled, and he pushed himself awkwardly upright, leaning against the back of the couch. "I'm not going anywhere!"

"We have to go now!" Farryn said. Cass watched him. His hands were clenched into fists, and he was rigid with tension, but she wasn't sure if he was keeping himself from punching his father, or from bursting into tears.

"I'm already dead, son," he said. He lay back down and closed his eyes. "You wanna drag around a corpse?"

"Cass," Farryn said quietly, without looking at her. "Check the bathroom drawers. There should be some antibiotic cream and bandages for Penny."

Cass hesitated, looking at Farryn, his shoulders slumped, standing over his father. She opened her mouth, then shut it. What could she say? She hurried to the bathroom and rifled through the drawers, finding the antibiotic and bandages, and also grabbing a pair of scissors that might be useful. She returned to the living room, where Farryn still stood over his motionless father.

"Dad," he said. "Please."

His father shook his head, eyes still closed, and said nothing.

Farryn stared down at his father. "Dad?" he said quietly.

"No," his father said.

Farryn unclenched his hands and turned away. "Let's go," he said to Cass.

"Farryn," said Cass, not sure what to say next, but he cut her off anyway.

"Leave him," Farryn said. "You heard him. We need to go."

Farryn had a streak of tears running down his cheeks as they left his father on the couch. Cass pretended not to notice.

CHAPTER 26

NICK AND LEXI HIKED NORTH WITH THE REBELS AND A HUNDRED CITY survivors, to the spot where they had gathered before the battle. Back at camp, Nick and Lexi circled around the survivors, who had been organized into two lines. No Cass. No Kevin.

"I should have stopped them," Nick said.

"They can take care of themselves, Nick," said Lexi. "It's not your fault."

"Yes, it is," Nick said.

He cut through the survivor lines, planning to do one more circuit of the camp—maybe he had missed them somehow—and then he stopped dead in his tracks in surprise. Sitting on a rock, next to the medic, holding something up to a survivor's neck, was Doc.

"Doc!" he said. Doc turned, looking around wildly, then

saw Nick and Lexi and stood. Surprisingly quick, he crossed the distance between them and crushed Nick and then Lexi in a strong, hairy-armed bear hug.

"You're alive!" Doc said. "Well done!"

Nick nodded. He was glad to see Doc, but his worry about his siblings was heavy on his mind. "Cass and Kevin . . . have you seen them?"

Doc frowned, and shook his head, "No, sorry," he said. "But tell me—"

He was cut off by Grennel, appearing from behind Nick, stepping between them and putting a hand on Doc's shoulder. Nick was startled; he hadn't heard the big man coming.

"The chip defusing is your only concern right now, doctor," Grennel said.

"It's just Doc," said Doc.

"Doc," Grennel repeated. "As I've told you, if we get word of any bot reinforcements, then we'll be leaving behind anyone who hasn't had their chip destroyed. Get busy."

"And I've told *you*, we're going to end up crippling someone, the way we're doing this." He pointed at Sarah, who was holding some sort of small device that looked like a wrench with a pyramid-shaped tip up to a survivor's neck. "It's barbaric. Some of these chips are too close to the spine. We can only control the radiation so much—"

"There's no time for any other way," Grennel said. "Do it, or we leave them behind."

Nick watched Sarah. She pressed a trigger on the device, and there was a pop, and the survivor, a middle-aged man, staggered forward a step and cried out. The back of his neck was blistered and red. Sarah quickly pressed an auto-injector into the burn, and the man's shoulders slumped with relief. She turned him around, and looked him in the eyes. The man nodded, then stepped away, and the next person in line stepped forward.

Doc glared at Grennel, then spun his substantial girth and went back to the rock.

Grennel turned to Nick. "Before you ask, yes, your brother is missing. And your sister and Farryn were supposed to stay in the camp, and they've disappeared. And we've just heard back from Rabbit and Moss—Erica escaped." Grennel folded his massive forearms over his chest. "Pretty soon nobody's going to be left. Do you know where any of them are?"

Nick shook his head. Cass and Kevin, gone. And Erica, escaped? What had happened with her?

Grennel lowered his voice. "The General is not happy. I'd avoid her right now, if I were you." He walked away.

Nick sat down, right there in the middle of all the chaos, and closed his eyes. *Kevin!* he said loudly, inside his head. *Where are you? Cass! Mom! Dad!* He strained for a response, for some sort of telepathic sense that they were okay, but of course he felt nothing. They were scattered, who knew where, yet again.

CHAPTER 27

KEVIN'S HEAD HURT, A THROBBING PAIN CENTERED IN THE BACK OF HIS skull that radiated around to his face and down his neck to his shoulders. He groaned and opened his eyes. The gray floor was cold on his left cheek. The floor hummed in his ear and vibrated gently. He pushed himself upright, and he felt a wave of dizziness that made him shut his eyes and brace his hands against the ground to keep from falling over.

The dizziness slowly ebbed and he opened his eyes again, breathing heavily. Where the hell was he? The room was small, a six-foot cube with gray walls, dimly lit by a light source that Kevin couldn't detect. There was absolutely nothing in the chamber—no furniture, no windows, no doors. It was an empty, sealed box. Empty, except for Kevin.

Kevin struggled to his feet and pushed against a wall. It was solid metal, cold and unyielding. He flung himself to the other wall, pounding on it with his fists, kicking. The walls were closing in . . . the ceiling was pushing down . . . he couldn't breathe . . . they had buried him alive. "Let me out!" he yelled. "Let me out!"

The floor disappeared, and the room was flooded with natural light. Kevin screamed, and tried to scramble up a wall. Below his feet were wispy clouds, and the green and brown earth, impossibly far down, rolling slowly past.

After the first moment of instinctive panic, thinking he was going to plunge down to his death, he stopped trying to climb the wall. He squatted down and gingerly felt for the floor. It was still there, solid cold metal beneath his feet, thrumming, but it was completely transparent. Or maybe it was a huge vidscreen, he thought, running his hand along the surface, his palm sliding above a wispy cloud. Far below, he could see the snaking blue line of a river, the gray crisscrossing lines of roadways, patches of green and brown and gray. Was this just a vid illusion? Or was he really thousands of feet in the sky?

"I thought you would appreciate the view," a voice said, originating from somewhere in the ceiling. It was a male voice, but the way the words were overly enunciated, the cadence just monotone enough to seem slightly strange, made Kevin immediately think, *Bot.*

Kevin pressed his back against a wall, still not comfortable to be standing over the floating sky. "Where are you taking me?" he said, looking up at the ceiling. He was proud of how steady his voice sounded. He certainly didn't feel very steady.

"Look down," the voice said. "We will be landing soon."

The plane—if Kevin really was in a plane, and not just being fooled by a vid—was much lower now, traveling over a gray, four-lane road that cut through an expanse of brown fields and lonely clumps of trees. They were only a few hundred feet off the ground now, traveling slowly, the road rolling quietly past. Was it possible that they had dropped so much altitude, so quickly, and Kevin hadn't even felt it?

"It is somewhat"—the voice paused—"old-fashioned . . . that our warbirds are equipped with cargo holds that allow for viewing, and contain gravitation countermands that negate any sensation of travel."

The voice seemed to be waiting for a response, but Kevin didn't say anything, and after a moment the voice continued. "A design holdover from the days, decades ago, when humans would physically pilot warbirds. It is . . . amusing . . . is it not, that this archaic design was never replaced?"

"No, not particularly," said Kevin.

"Perhaps not," said the voice. "Humor is a complicated human trait that is surprisingly elusive. I have yet to devote much time to the subject."

Kevin didn't know what to say to that, but then the road

below his feet ended, and the warbird came to a hovering halt over a large square plain of dull gray metal. The warbird lowered down, and a crack appeared in the landing field, quickly separating into a gaping hole, the two sides of the field sliding away to reveal a clean white shaft, lit with the harsh artificial glow of strong lightstrips. The floor of the shaft was marked with a red *X*, and the warbird eased down toward the center of the X, coming to a halt with the intersection of the lines directly below Kevin's feet.

"Welcome to City 1," the voice said. "I look forward to meeting you in the flesh."

The floor darkened, becoming just gray metal again, and then a vertical line appeared in one of the walls. The two sections of the wall separated, with just the slightest hiss of sound. Two bots stood at the top of a ramp that led down ten feet from the cargo hold to the floor of the landing shaft. They were similar to the Island's bots, but a bit taller, and bulkier, and of course their skin was unbroken white neo-plas, without any cured leather patches.

Kevin retreated to the back of the cargo hold. He had his hands up, raised in fists, which he realized was ridiculous. He dropped his hands, but didn't move.

"Come with us." The voice came from the bot on the left, although its mouth slit didn't move.

"Go rust yourselves," said Kevin.

"We have been authorized to use force to transport you,"

said the other bot. "We will not cause lasting damage, but we will cause pain. Will coercion be required?"

"No," said Kevin. He didn't have much choice; he might as well avoid the pain. "No coercion required."

The bots led him out of the landing shaft, one in front, one behind, and down a long white-tiled corridor. They entered an elevator, rode it for a few seconds, then emerged into another seemingly identical hallway. They led him to a door, and one of the bots pressed its hand against a control plate. The door retracted into the wall.

The old man inside the room, wearing a tan jumpsuit, stood up. Kevin froze, dumbfounded.

"Hello, Kevin," said Dr. Miles Winston. "I am so, so sorry to see you."

CHAPTER 28

CASS LAY ON THE GRASS, WIDE AWAKE, WATCHING HER PARENTS AND
Penny sleep. It was a warm night, but the three were huddled
together, and as Cass watched them, she realized that Penny
may have never slept outdoors in her entire life. Her parents,
too—maybe in their lives before the City, before their complete
re-education, they had camped—but certainly since becoming
Hightowners, they hadn't slept anywhere but their comfortable apartment.

Cass felt guilty for what they were going to face. Logically
she knew it wasn't her fault—they couldn't stay in the City,
and they couldn't join Clay—but still, she felt like all the suf-
fering coming their way was indeed because of her, somehow.
What was it Clay had said? *I'm a leader. I decide. I act. I don't*

get distracted by tangential details or collateral damage. Cass wished it were that simple for her.

She lay there, worrying, trying to come up with a plan, and then Farryn began thrashing in his sleep, groaning and muttering. Had his fever come back? Had she pushed him too hard? Cass stood and quietly crossed the few steps between them. She gently felt his forehead—it was cool and dry. She gave a sigh of relief. No fever—just a nightmare.

If she could ever get to sleep, she'd probably be having nightmares, too, after what they had just gone through. She looked down at Farryn. He had to be exhausted, and hurting, but he had kept up as best he could. He was so brave. Would she have been able to keep going, the way he had, if she had lost a leg? She doubted it.

And somehow, for some reason, he was trying to help her, to protect her. She sighed. More responsibility. Farryn would never see it that way, of course, but if she was going to lead him into trouble, and he got hurt even more, or killed, it would be her fault.

Farryn opened his eyes. "Cass?" he said, disoriented.

Embarrassed, Cass quickly stood. "Go back to sleep," she said.

"What . . ." he said. "What are you doing?"

"Nothing." Cass sat down on the ground. Farryn rolled over to face her, and waited.

"I'm thinking," she said. "And worrying."

Farryn smiled, a sleepy, half-awake smile. "What've you

got to worry about? Your life couldn't be easier."

"Yeah, right," Cass said, smiling back at him, surprised at how easily he cheered her up. But the feeling didn't last long, and she felt her smile fade. She nodded in the direction of her sleeping family. "They're going to have a hard time away from the City. I don't know how they're going to manage."

"We'll find a Freepost for them," said Farryn. "We've got supplies for a few days, and you can hunt. It'll be okay."

"I want you to leave," Cass said. "Go back to Clay."

Farryn sat up. "What are you talking about?" he said. He looked, Cass thought, like she had slapped him. His expression made her feel even worse.

"It's not safe," Cass said. "It's a stupid, dangerous thing I'm doing, and you don't have to be a part of it."

Farryn's face relaxed, and he lay back down. "Scared me there for a minute. Sorry, Cass. You're stuck with me."

"But . . ." Cass began.

Farryn rolled over, turning his back to her. "Nope. I'm done listening. Going back to sleep now. You can scratch my back if you want to, but no more talking."

Cass stood. She couldn't help smiling. "You're as stubborn as I am, aren't you?" she said.

"Worse," said Farryn. "Now how about that back scratch?"

"Not happening," she said. She returned to her bedroll, lay down, and within seconds was in a deep, dreamless sleep.

* * *

The morning sun woke her. Farryn was already up, stretching. She stood, doing a few stretches of her own, noticing that Farryn was watching her while pretending not to. She went to wake her family, shaking her parents, and then Penny, gently on the shoulder.

Penny got up quickly, fresh like she had spent the night in a soft bed, while her parents struggled slowly to their feet, obviously stiff and uncomfortable. Cass's father massaged his lower back. Cass examined Penny's cuts—they looked good, no sign of infection. She spread a thin layer of antibiotic cream on Penny's cheek and forearm, and put a fresh bandage on the arm gash.

"We should get moving," Cass said. "We can eat while we walk."

Penny suddenly looked uncomfortable. She glanced at Farryn, then leaned toward Cass and whispered, "I have to go to the bathroom. What do I do?"

Cass had to force herself not to laugh. She didn't want Penny to think she was making fun of her. Cass pointed at the trees. "Find a tree. Go behind it. Use leaves if you need to."

Penny just stared at her, wide-eyed, and then Cass went ahead and laughed; she couldn't help it. "Go! Hurry up. You'll survive."

Penny glanced at her mother, who nodded, and she walked a short ways into the woods and ducked behind a tree. Thirty seconds later she returned, grinning. "That was the strangest thing I've ever done," she said.

"Cass," her father said, "where are you proposing we go? I think perhaps we should stay put, and wait for the robot advisors to reclaim the City."

Stay put? Rust, her father really didn't understand. "We can't stay here," she said, trying not to sound annoyed. "The City's not safe, and I don't know if your bots are coming back, and we're too close to Clay's rebels."

"Who are these rebels?" her mother said. "Why did they destroy our City?"

"They're trying to take it back," Cass said. "For humans." She thought of the fires, the collapsed buildings, the dead bodies, and her words sounded hollow in her ears. "But you're—" She paused, about to call them "True Believers."

"You're *partners* with the bots, you're true citizens, and the rebels, especially their leader, wouldn't like that." She looked at Penny, considered sugarcoating it, then decided on the truth. "They'd probably kill you."

Her mother paled, and her father looked grim. He put his arm over Penny's shoulders. "Then we'll get to the nearest City. It's northeast of here, I know that much, but I'm not sure how far. We'll find a road; we'll hopefully be able to flag down a robot transport of some sort. . . ."

Cass looked at Farryn, who shook his head and raised his hands, as if to say, *I have no idea what you should tell him.* She looked back at her father.

"It's not . . . it's not that simple," she said. "We've attacked the bots. They're probably going to assume any humans they find are rebels."

"We'll explain," her father said.

"You'll have a lase blast in your chest before you have the chance to say anything," Cass said angrily. She took a breath, then continued more calmly, "And Farryn and I . . . the bots will definitely kill us."

Cass's father shook his head, and ran his hands through his hair. "Will you help us get to the northeast? To the other City?"

Cass nodded. "We'll be staying away from the roads, though. We need to avoid bots and rebels." It was a start. At least they'd be moving. And it would give her time to find a Freepost, and figure out how to change her parents' minds.

CHAPTER 29

IT WAS SARAH, NOT DOC, WHO KILLED SOMEONE WHILE BURNING OUT chip implants. Nick was sitting fifteen feet away when it happened and had a clear view of the woman's face when she died. She was short, with strikingly sharp blue eyes and long brown hair that had just a few streaks of gray. She was probably in her late forties, perhaps early fifties. She screamed when Sarah touched her neck—that wasn't unusual—but instead of the small pop that others had experienced, her chip blew with a loud bang and a flare of flame that singed her hair. She convulsed in a wave that rolled through her entire body, her blue eyes rolled up in her head, and she collapsed. It wasn't a soft fall; it was as if her bones had suddenly left her body and she just crumpled, hard and fast, facedown in the dirt.

Sarah and Doc, after flinching from the blast, quickly went to work on her, taking her pulse, examining the wound on the back of her neck. The remaining survivors in line watched, stricken. A few cried quietly, their hands over their mouths. Others just stood silent and ashen-faced. Nick found himself on his feet and halfway to the woman before he stopped himself. What could he possibly do that the medic and Doc couldn't?

Doc swore, and stood. "I told her!" he said to Sarah. "I told her this would happen!"

Sarah didn't say anything. She rolled the dead woman onto her back and closed her eyes with her fingers.

The City survivors still in line were upset. Nick could hear someone saying, "No! No way in hell am I going to let them do that to me!" Others muttered their agreement, and the lines began to disperse.

"Hold!" said Clay to the group, walking quickly to the dead woman. Grennel followed. The survivors hesitated, not reforming lines, but staying put.

Clay looked down at the dead woman, then turned to Sarah. "What happened here?" she said.

"I'll tell you what happened," said Doc angrily, stepping forward. Grennel moved closer to Clay, but Doc didn't seem to notice. "Her chip shorted too strongly from this damned procedure you're forcing us to do, and it severed her spine and we killed her." Doc's fists were clenched. "You killed her."

"Calm yourself," said Clay quietly. "You don't want to upset the new recruits unnecessarily."

Doc took a step toward Clay, but Grennel reached out and put a hand on Doc's shoulder, and casually, as if he wasn't even exerting any effort, stopped Doc in his tracks. Nick quietly moved closer. He knew there wasn't much he'd be able to do in a fight against Grennel, but if Doc needed his help, he'd certainly try.

Doc looked up at Grennel, as if noticing the huge man for the first time. Nick relaxed a bit when Grennel let Doc step back, out from under his grip. Doc lowered his voice, to match Clay's. "It was this poor woman dying that upset folks, not the tone of my voice."

"Enough of this," Clay said. She turned to the group of City survivors and raised her voice. "This is extremely regrettable," she said to the group. "This procedure is not without some risks."

"You call that 'some risks'?" a tall, blond man said, pointing down at the dead woman.

Clay said nothing, staring at the man who had interrupted. The man held her gaze for a few moments, then his defiance shifted to discomfort and he looked away.

"Yes," Clay continued. "There are some risks. But these are necessary risks, and the complications are rare." She paused. "I don't wish to sound callous, but the accident that just occurred means it is statistically very unlikely that the incident will be repeated."

Doc looked like he wanted to speak, but Clay shot him a look, and he said nothing. Instead he turned and walked stiffly away. Clay watched him leave, a slight clenching of her jaw the only sign that she was displeased.

"What if we refuse?" said the blond man.

"Then you will leave my camp immediately," said Clay.

"And go where?" said the man.

Clay shrugged. "Go back to the City. Search for a Freepost in the woods. I don't care. But stay away from my forces. If you come near any of my camps with that chip still in your neck, I'll have you shot and burned."

The man paled. There was silence.

Grennel stepped in front of Clay. "Come," he said, addressing the survivors. "Join us, please. If you choose to leave, you may leave freely. But I hope you will be brave, and have your chips neutralized, and stay with us to fight."

Grennel's broad frame blocked Clay from the group, but Nick could clearly see the flash of rage on her face and the clenching of her fists. Apparently, Nick realized, she didn't appreciate Grennel's interruption. She quickly mastered her anger, straightening her fingers and relaxing her face.

Nick went looking for Doc, finding him sitting on a rock, looking south toward the City. A few fires still flickered in the distance. He was leaning forward, his hands clasped together, his thick forearms resting on his thighs. It almost looked like he was praying. He straightened up when Nick approached.

"She's bad news, Nick," he said. "If she's our champion, then we're in for a bumpy revolution."

"No doubt," Nick said. He sat down on the ground next to the rock. "It's good to see you, Doc," he said. "I'm glad you're okay."

"And you," Doc said. "Your sister and your brother, are they okay? And Farryn and Lexi?"

Nick found himself about to choke up, and he had to take a few seconds to gain control before responding. "Lexi and Farryn found us. Lexi's here in the camp. Farryn . . . he lost a leg, bot blast, but he's with my sister now, and I don't know where they are. Kevin's gone, too." He paused, and Doc waited patiently. "I lost them," Nick finally continued. "Again. They both went into the City. Cass was trying to find her birth parents, and Kevin . . . he had some tech that he thought would keep him safe, and he went to get Mom and Dad."

"They are stubborn, and resourceful," Doc said. "They'll survive, I suspect."

Nick couldn't get any words out; he just nodded. They sat in silence, looking at the City, and then Nick cleared his throat and said, "My parents? Are they okay? Do you know?"

"After you left I replaced your father's false chip successfully. They left my apartment soon after. I'm sorry, but I haven't seen them since." Doc paused, then said, "Tell me, Nick, did you make it to the Freepost to the north? Did you . . . did you meet the mayor? And her son? Did they get my pigeon?"

Nick felt his stomach twist. He had been dreading this. "Yes, thank you very much. I made it to the Freepost, and I met her . . . your wife. And your son."

Doc smiled sadly. "How is she? Probably annoyed that she hasn't heard from me in so long? It's a big risk, you know, sending one of the Freepost birds. If the bots somehow discovered . . . I was keeping her safe, by not keeping in touch. And my son . . . is he still a big strong blockhead?"

Doc's face fell when he saw Nick's hesitation. "Tell me," he said. Nick sighed. "Now," Doc said.

"They were well, and they asked about you . . . but . . ."

"Rust, boy, just spit it out!"

"The Freepost was attacked the day after I arrived. I got away, but it was pretty bad. I don't know what happened to your wife or son. I'm sorry," Nick said, feeling guilt wash over him. "I should have stayed and fought."

Doc shook his head angrily. "Then you'd be dead or captured, too," he said. He scratched his forehead, then rested his head in his hands a moment, before sighing and looking back up at Nick. "They're tough, too, just like Kevin and Cass. All we can do is trust they will survive. Hell, maybe they're better off away from this Clay woman anyway."

CHAPTER 30

KEVIN WAS SO SHOCKED HE JUST STOOD IN THE DOORWAY, HIS MOUTH agape. One of the bots pushed him on the back, not quite a shove, but hard enough to send him into the room. The door slid shut behind him.

"Grandfather?" he said quietly. "But . . . you were killed . . . I saw Grennel shoot you. . . ."

"Shot, yes—killed, no," said Dr. Winston. "I thought I was dead, Kevin. I don't remember much . . . just the pain, passing out, and then I woke up in a rejuve tank." He frowned and looked away. "Unfortunately," he added quietly. "It would have been better for both of us if I had indeed died on the floor of my lab."

"What do they want?" said Kevin, not really wanting to know the answer. "What are they going to do to us?"

"Two very different questions," said Dr. Winston. He sat down on the metal bed. "What they want is for me to help them bypass their replication block." He looked at the wall, hands in his lap, lost in thought.

Kevin waited for an explanation, then, exasperated, asked, "What's that? The replication block?"

Dr. Winston started. "Yes, of course . . . sorry . . . I'm a foolish old man, lost in my thoughts." He patted the bed next to him. "Sit," he said, then continued. "About ten years before the revolution—it was 2042, I think—our warbot artificial intelligence had advanced to the point where the bots had begun to design and implement their own improvements. I was called back into service—I hadn't worked for the military in years at that point—because the generals and politicians were spooked.

"It was an incident in Asia that did it. We had a field factory out there, near where we were fighting about something . . . I can't even remember what about. Maybe the Chinese were invading India again?" His eyes unfocused for a moment, then he shrugged. "Anyway, we negotiated a cease-fire but there was a comm failure and we couldn't stand down the bots remotely, and when crews arrived they found that they had no idea how to manually shut down the bots.

"The new models, you see—designed and crafted by the bots themselves—had designed away their failsafes." Dr. Winston paused.

"And?" said Kevin. "What did you do?"

Dr. Winston waved his hands dismissively. "Eventually the bots stood themselves down. But like I said, I was brought in, and I worked with Harrington, Chesnick, and a few others to design the replication block code.

"Long story short, lots of interesting coding, then diplomatic back and forth to get the major powers to buy in—but it wasn't just us; everyone was spooked by the bots birthing uncontrollable versions of themselves. So a year later we had a worldwide implementation of our code, which made it impossible for a robot to create another artificial life form by itself. We built in lots of roadblocks, too, hoops for the military to jump through to create more warbots even with human approval. I was quite proud of myself at the time, actually." He shook his head ruefully. "Considered myself quite the peacemonger."

"So the bots now . . . they can't build more of themselves?"

Dr. Winston nodded. "Correct. They can't remove the code, and they can't replicate. That's one of my justifications for building the Island, actually. I believed if I could just survive long enough, the robots would slowly diminish in numbers, as others fought. You were right," he said. "I was a coward."

Kevin shook his head, but he couldn't get himself to disagree out loud. His grandfather had indeed been a coward.

Dr. Winston, waiting, watching Kevin, then frowned sadly and looked away. "And as for your second question," he said, "what they're going to do with us . . . well, they're going to use you as leverage to get me to help defuse the code. And after they get what they need, they're going to re-educate us, or kill us."

Kevin was suddenly very afraid. He stood up, but his legs felt rubbery, so he sat back down. "Which one's worse?" he whispered.

"What do you mean?" said Dr. Winston.

"Death or re-education?" said Kevin.

Dr. Winston stood. "I am sorry, Kevin. I can be thoughtless. I am not good with people, not even family." He put his hand on Kevin's shoulder. "Neither will happen. You will not be killed. You will not be re-educated. Understood? I will find a way to protect you."

Kevin nodded weakly.

"You don't believe me," said Dr. Winston.

"No," said Kevin. "I don't."

"Say it, Kevin. Say, 'I will not be killed.'"

"I will not be killed," Kevin whispered.

"I will not be re-educated."

"I will not be re-educated," Kevin repeated. Dr. Winston nodded, satisfied, but Kevin still didn't believe it.

CHAPTER 31

"RUST," SAID LEXI. "ISN'T THERE SOMETHING WE CAN DO?"

The seven survivors who refused to submit to the de-chipping procedure left the temporary camp, heading north, away from the City. Nick watched them go, feeling helpless and angry. They were probably going to get killed, but what could he do for them? Insist that Clay let them stay? That would certainly go over well.

"No," he said to Lexi angrily. He felt like a coward, and he was mad at himself, but it came out sounding like he was mad at her. Lexi raised her eyebrows at him, and walked away to talk to Doc. Nick thought about how to apologize, or explain . . . but it was complicated.

He heard the crunch of approaching footsteps, and turned

to see Ro coming his way, along with Rabbit. The gash Ro had received in the City had turned into a jagged pink scar. Rabbit looked worse. He had a black eye and his nose was crooked and swollen. Nick suppressed a smile. Erica had really done a number on him, apparently, when she escaped.

"Come with me," Ro said. Nick thought, *Hell, what now?* but followed Ro and Rabbit to a quiet spot behind one of the collapsed buildings. "Were you involved in any way in Erica's escape?" Ro said abruptly. "Do you know anything about her plans?"

Taken by surprise, Nick shook his head. "No," he said. "That Erica's work?" he said to Rabbit, nodding at the man's bruised face.

Rabbit scowled. "He must know something," he said to Ro. "I'm telling you, he was soft for her."

Ro stared at Nick, saying nothing else. Nick folded his arms over his chest and stared back. Ro nodded at Rabbit. "Go," he said.

With one more glare at Nick, Rabbit walked away.

Ro watched him leave, then turned back to Nick. "I believe you," he said. "But the General is going to have questions, when things settle down enough for her to bother. Rabbit is right, I know you have some sympathy for Erica." Nick started to protest, and Ro held up his hand and cut him off. "Think," he said. "Do you have any idea where she may have gone?"

"I don't know," Nick said. "I know she was worried about

her brother, especially after our attack, when the bots would realize she had given them bad intel . . . but I have no idea where she went."

"And your sister?" said Ro. "And Farryn? And your brother?"

"I don't know," Nick said, his voice catching in his throat. "They went into the battle, I think. I don't know."

"Clay's not happy," said Ro. "Especially about Kevin."

Nick wanted to say something like *Clay can go rust herself*, but he kept his mouth shut.

"You're running out of people," Ro said.

"Yes," Nick said quietly. "Yes, I am."

Ro shook his head, then began walking away. "Come on," he said. "Help me organize the survivors. We're headed for better cover."

The rebels quickly organized the City survivors, and led them north an hour, deeper into forest cover. They waited there for a day, Ro assessing the skills of the new recruits, Nick growing more and more agitated. He couldn't just hide in the woods, doing nothing.

The next morning two scouts returned from the south, disappearing into Clay's tent with Ro and Grennel. They reemerged after a half hour, and soon after the word filtered down through Ro's lieutenants to the rest of the rebels—there had been no sign of bot reinforcement from other cities. No air support. No land support. Nothing.

Why? Everyone in camp was speculating. Some thought the bots didn't care about City 73, and were saving their resources for more important Cities. Nick heard someone say that the bots were cowards, and now that they had a real fight on their hands, they were running scared. Another rumor was that the bots' communication network was somehow down, so they couldn't organize. And quietly, a few were saying that perhaps it was a trap, that the bots were waiting for the rebels to overreach, and then they would really show their numbers.

None of it sounded quite right to Nick, although he didn't have any better ideas. Maybe Erica's false intel had worked even better than they had hoped?

And then the orders came down . . . they were going to push forward . . . first a quick recon back to City 73 to gather supplies, then a march to the northwest, to take on another City.

Apparently, thought Nick, *we're going to press our luck.*

CHAPTER 32

HER PARENTS AND SISTER, TO CASS'S EARS, SOUNDED LIKE ELEPHANTS when they walked. It was as if they were going out of their way to step on every branch, kick every pebble, crunch every leaf, splash in every drop of water. She knew it wasn't their fault—they knew nothing about traveling outside the City—but it still grated on Cass's nerves. A good tracker, human or bot, would hear them coming a hundred yards away.

She had asked them once to try to be more quiet, and they had looked shocked, then tried their best. It was almost comical, the way they began picking their way like they were walking through a minefield. Their pace was so slow that she soon told them not to worry about it. Even doing their mine-field walk, they were still noisy.

Farryn, his gait stiff on the right side because of his fake leg, somehow managed to be fairly quiet. He didn't sound like a Freeposter, certainly, but he did surprisingly well. "You're a City boy," she whispered to Farryn, loud enough for only him to hear. "How'd you learn to walk so quietly?"

Farryn shrugged. "Learned from you, I guess. I've done a lot of watching you walk."

Cass, flustered, couldn't come up with a witty reply, so she dropped back to check on her parents and Penny. Her parents looked tired. Her mother had a scratch on her cheek from a tree branch, and her father had torn the sleeve of his shirt. Penny, on the other hand, looked fresh, and she smiled when Cass began walking beside her.

"It's different than I imagined," Penny said. She waved her hands at the trees. "The wilderness, I mean. It's not as . . . not as wild, I guess."

"We're still close to the City," Cass said. "There's not much forest yet." They were just a few miles outside the City, and the terrain was mostly roads and abandoned pre-Rev buildings, with only patchy tree cover.

Penny's face fell. "Oh, yeah, of course. I'm an idiot."

Cass felt terrible. "No! It wasn't stupid. . . . I mean, you've never even been outside the City, so how would you know? You're doing great, actually. It's amazing how well you're doing."

Penny's face lit up again. "Thanks, Cass."

Cass's mother smiled weakly at the exchange, but her father remained grim-faced.

They broke for lunch, resting on the bank of a ravine. They were still close to a roadway, and without much cover. Cass would have preferred to keep walking, but she knew that her parents needed a rest. At least the ravine bank helped a little— they would be able to see someone, or something, coming on the road while still hidden.

Lunch consisted of two packs of noodles taken from her parents' kitchen, boiled in a pot of water over a very small fire. The noodles didn't properly hydrate—they had been designed for a City hydrator, not a campfire. They were crunchy, but edible.

"Have you ever had squirrel?" Farryn asked Penny.

Penny shook her head, her eyes wide.

"It's better than you'd think. Especially when I cook it," he said. He leaned forward. "Cass tends to burn it," he said in a mock whisper.

"Farryn," Cass began, and then she saw the movement, off in the distance on the road, and she hissed, "Down! Everyone down! Stay quiet!"

Farryn hit the ground, followed a moment later by Cass's father and mother, who pulled a bewildered Penny down to the grass.

"Stay down," Cass whispered. She peered over the edge of the ravine bank. There—yes, she hadn't been imagining it—a group of people was coming up the road, moving north, from the direction of the City. *Are they rebels?* she wondered. But what were they doing walking openly on the road? And then with a flutter of fear she thought, *Could they be humanoid bots, like the Lecturers?* But no, as they slowly drew closer, she could see that they walked like people, and she began to make out details. There were seven of them—three women and four men. They wore City clothing—the bright colors of the women's dresses had been what had caught Cass's eye. They had no weapons that Cass could see, certainly no rifles. Only a few carried any gear at all—two of the men had plastic sacks slung awkwardly over their shoulders. They trudged up the middle of the road, keeping a decent pace, although they looked weary. Cass could hear their footsteps and the scraping of pebbles.

Farryn crawled up to the lip of the ridge, joining her to her left, and then, more loudly, her father crawled up on Cass's right.

"I said stay down," she whispered to both of them, annoyed.

"They're from the City," her father said, ignoring her, and he began to rise. Cass grabbed his shirt, and, surprising herself with her own strength, yanked him roughly back down.

"No!" she whispered. "Not safe!"

Her father glared at her, but she held on to his shirt. "They'll get us killed," she said. Her father's angry expression faded, and he blinked slowly, then nodded. She let go of his shirt. He stayed down.

They watched the group come closer and closer, eventually passing by within thirty feet of them. The group never once looked in their direction. The seven of them kept their eyes grimly up the road. They looked tired. One of the men was walking with a slight limp.

Blindly marching up the road, making all that noise, with their bright colors . . . *How long would it take for them to be captured by bots, or discovered by the rebels?* Cass wondered. She knew she couldn't get involved with these survivors— she'd never be able to feed them all, and with their obvious lack of wilderness skills, they'd be a beacon for any enemies within miles. She had to look out for herself, and her family, didn't she? Still, she felt guilty and selfish as she watched them slowly disappear up the road.

CHAPTER 33

"WELCOME!" THE BOT SAID, STANDING UP FROM WHERE IT SAT AT A long rectangular table in an otherwise empty room. Kevin recognized the voice—it was the bot who had spoken to him when he was trapped in the cargo hold of the warbird.

It looked nearly human—it was about six feet tall, with properly proportioned limbs, and its face had cheekbones and a mouth that moved when it talked. The nose, eyes, and ears were strikingly lifelike. The facial features were just a bit soft, though, less defined than an actual person, as if they were created by an amateur sculptor who almost but couldn't quite manage realism. And then there was the skin, of course, which was stark, fish-belly white.

The bot wore a broad-shouldered, military-cut black shirt

and matching black trousers that made the inhuman white-ness of its skin seem even harsher. When it stepped away from the table, Kevin was surprised to see that it wore a pair of broken-in, scuffed leather hiking boots, incongruously and utterly human.

The bot smiled at Kevin and his grandfather, or rather gave an unsettling approximation of a smile—its facial muscles remained too rigid, and the rest of the face was oddly unaf-fected by the movement of the mouth. "I see you have noticed my boots," it said to Kevin. "These came from a human who failed re-education and no longer had need of them. They are an affectation, perhaps, but nevertheless, I appreciate the qual-ity of the construction. They are a reminder, to me, of both the frailty of humanity—that you need to protect your feet from the elements—and your ingenuity in adaptation."

"I have no idea what you're talking about," said Kevin. "They're a pair of shoes that you stole from a guy you killed."

Dr. Winston chuckled. The bot looked at him, blank-faced, then turned back to Kevin. "I digress," it said. "Kevin, I am the Senior Advisor. Your grandfather and I, over the past few days, have already had the opportunity to get to know each other. Now it is your turn."

Kevin felt the hairs on the back of his neck stand up. He had to fight the instinct to step back, to create more distance between himself and the bot.

"Leave him alone," Dr. Winston said angrily.

"Dr. Winston, *Father*, be calm."

"I'm not your father," said Dr. Winston.

"You designed me," said the Senior Advisor. "You gave me a level of self-awareness and cognition unmatched by any other synthetic intelligence."

"It was a team of us, not just me," said Dr. Winston. "And your advanced processing was supposed to be for advanced tactical planning, not"—Dr. Winston paused—"not this. Not revolution. You were designed to serve humans."

"I do serve them, Father. I do. For example, now I will serve you a meal." The bot nodded at the table, and Kevin noticed for the first time that the corner of the table was set with three place settings. "That was a play on words, Father. Humor, I believe."

"No, I believe not," said Kevin.

"Regardless," said the Senior Advisor, "sit."

"No, thank you," said Dr. Winston.

"Yeah, not hungry," said Kevin, although he was actually famished.

The Senior Advisor sat down at the end of the table. Dr. Winston and Kevin remained standing. The door behind them opened, and a guard bot stepped in. The door shut behind it.

"Sit down," said the Senior Advisor. "Or you will be forced to sit, and that will be painful for you."

Kevin looked at his grandfather, who nodded and moved to the table. Kevin followed, and sat.

"There," said the Senior Advisor, smiling again and making Kevin feel like flinching. "A family meal. Pleasant."

The guard bot left the room, then reappeared after a few uncomfortable moments of silence, pushing a tray laden with three plates. The dishes were beautiful—even Kevin noticed. They were white porcelain, with a line of gold around the rim. On each plate was a steak with a brown mushroom sauce, a baked potato with sour cream and chives, and asparagus. The guard set the plates down in front of the three, filled Kevin's and Dr. Winston's glasses with water, then left the room.

"Eat," said the Senior Advisor.

Kevin dug in to the meal. He hadn't eaten in a long time, too long, and he was starving. He wasn't going to pass up the opportunity, no matter how strange the circumstances. They probably wouldn't bother poisoning him, he reasoned. Seemed like too much trouble, when they could just lase him if they felt like it.

While Kevin attacked his steak, Dr. Winston took a small bite of baked potato, then sipped his water, keeping a wary eye on the Senior Advisor.

The Senior Advisor cut a piece of steak, chewed it thoughtfully, then leaned over and gently spit it into a side dish. Kevin paused in the inhalation of his food, staring at the pink, half-chewed meat.

"It has no digestive system," said Dr. Winston to Kevin. "It can't swallow. It doesn't need food."

"That is correct," said the Senior Advisor. He tasted the baked potato, spitting it next to the chewed steak, then did the same with the asparagus.

"So what the hell are you doing?" said Kevin, disgusted.

The Senior Advisor set his utensils down. "I am experiencing the food," he said.

"Yeah, well, that's special," Kevin said.

"You are maintaining a facade of defiance, I note," said the Senior Advisor. "Is this for my benefit, or your own? Is your intention to impress me with your supposed lack of concern, or to bolster your own confidence?"

Kevin shook his head. "You're just stringing big words together, I think."

The Senior Advisor smiled suddenly, and this time Kevin couldn't help it—he actually did flinch, leaning back in his seat, before catching himself. The bot stood and turned away, clasping its hands behind its back. "Dr. Winston," it said, facing the wall, "do you know why I brought Kevin here?"

Dr. Winston picked up his steak knife, and turned to the bot. Kevin tensed, and wanted to say, *No, don't*, but he kept quiet. Could the bot really be damaged with the knife? If anyone would know, his grandfather would. This bot wasn't armored like a Petey. . . . Maybe a strong jab and cut, in the right spot on the neck, would quickly sever the main motor control and comm wiring.

Dr. Winston began to stand, still holding the knife, and

Kevin held his breath. His grandfather's hand was shaking—
Kevin could see the knife quivering—and then Dr. Winston
sat back down heavily and let the knife drop to the table. He
put his head in his hands.

Kevin let his breath out, feeling slightly dizzy. He wasn't
sure if he was disappointed or relieved.

The Senior Advisor turned back to the table, seemingly
oblivious to the moment of drama. "Motivation," he said. He
put his hands on the table and leaned forward, toward Dr.
Winston. "I can continue to hurt you, but there is only so
much your elderly body will withstand, and multiple rejuve-
nations are not an option for someone of your age. We would
most likely kill you unintentionally, or merely extract false
promises." He stood back up, and nodded at Kevin. "However,
I am a student, as you know, *Father*, of human relationships,
and I suspect that watching your grandson suffer would provide strong incentive for you to cooperate."

Kevin felt as if his heart stopped beating. He couldn't feel
his fingers or his toes.

"Am I correct?" the Senior Advisor said.

Dr. Winston nodded, his eyes glistening.

"Grandfather, no," Kevin whispered.

"It's okay, Kevin," said Dr. Winston. "It'll be okay. Trust me."

"So you will help us disable our reproduction block
code?" said the Senior Advisor. "I am tired of conserving my
resources. There are flies I wish to swat."

Dr. Winston said nothing.

"Father?" said the Senior Advisor.

"I will," said Dr. Winston quietly.

"Excellent," said the Senior Advisor, returning to his chair. "Now, how about dessert?"

CHAPTER 34

CASS LED FARRYN AND HER FAMILY NORTHWEST FOR FOUR DAYS. FARRYN grew stronger, and more confident on his prosthetic leg, each day. Penny also, considering she was born and raised in a City, did amazingly well. By the second day she was moving much more quietly, and by the third day she even helped Cass scout ahead and hunt for squirrel.

Her parents, on the other hand, grew more fatigued, and if possible, even clumsier. They barely spoke. Her father wore a bleak expression on his face that never eased, and her mother, who at first had tried to offer a forced sense of optimism, had eventually given up and lapsed into a blank-faced exhaustion.

Cass had tried, once, to broach the subject of their destination—did it really make sense for them to go to another City?

she had asked—but her father, animated for the first time in a day, had immediately grown angry.

"Of course! What are we going to do, live out here like wildmen, waiting for rebels or the plague to kill us?"

"There's no such thing as the plague," Cass had said weakly, and her father just scowled and shook his head.

She tried, as they hiked, to come up with a way to keep them away from the new City. She wanted them in a Freepost, living free from the bots. But a small part of her—a part that she hated but couldn't get to shut up—wondered if they would actually be better off in a City. The City life, bot control, was what they knew. Was she making a mistake, trying to force them away from the life that made them happy?

On the morning of the fourth day, they crested a long, low hill, and looked down into a valley at a City, a half mile away. It was smaller than City 73—most of the buildings were one- and two-story white structures, bot-design, except for the center of the City, which contained a nucleus of taller, pre-Rev buildings.

Her father let out a whoop of joy, and hugged his wife, who Cass saw was crying. Cass watched them, saddened, but also happy for them. This would be their home, she realized. This is what they needed. She'd say good-bye to them here on this crest, and watch them walk down into the valley and enter the City, and then she'd never see them again.

Cass was still looking at her parents when the first bomb exploded. She saw the flash of light reflect on their faces, saw their eyes open wide in shock, and then heard the rumble. She spun and saw the flames in the center of the City, a pre-Rev building crumbling. Another explosion rocked the City, this time on the northern outskirts, among the low white structures, and then a third, back in the City center.

She instinctively dropped to the ground. Farryn was beside her, and Penny on the other side, but her parents just stood there, still holding each other, their joy turned to horror.

The explosions lasted fifteen minutes. They could see and hear lase flashes. They all watched, silently. It had to be Clay, Cass knew. She was taking the fight to other Cities. *Is Nick down there fighting?* she wondered. *Kevin?*

Cass stood up, brushing the dirt off her shirt and pants. "Come on," she said to her parents, who were still reluctant to move. "It's not safe here."

"We'll find another City," whispered her father, his eyes still fixed on the burning City below. "I know there're more, I just don't know where. . . ."

"The Cities aren't safe for you anymore," said Cass. She waved her arm angrily at the valley. "Can't you see that?"

Her father tore his eyes away from the destruction and stared at Cass blankly. "Then where? Where do we go?"

"I'll find a Freepost," Cass said. "I'll get you somewhere safe."

"It'll be okay," Penny said, tugging on her parents. "I trust Cass. Let's go."

Her mother grabbed Penny and crushed her in a tight, brief hug, and her father nodded almost imperceptibly at Cass, looking lost and defeated. "Okay, Cass," he said. "Find us a Freepost."

CHAPTER 35

NICK WAS GIVEN DOUBLE SHIFTS OF SENTRY DUTIES, LEAVING HIM ONLY a few hours of sleep each night, and he was exhausted. "Get used to it," Ro told him. "General Clay won't be letting you get much rest unless your brother and sister and Erica come back. You're lucky she's not doing anything worse than just some sleep deprivation."

Thankfully they still let him fight—he had proven to be too good a soldier to be sidelined. Over the next two weeks, the rebels invaded two more Cities. Each was a repeat of City 73—the camouflaged rebels snuck in first, taking out bot administration and comm targets, and then the rebels swept in for the cleanup. Rebels died, but not many, and Clay's forces grew stronger, gaining food and weapons and medicine and recruits.

It was too easy, Nick thought. It felt wrong. There just weren't enough bots in the Cities to put up much of a fight. Were the bots stretched too thin? Were the rebel victories so insignificant that the bot leaders hadn't even been paying attention?

Nick worried that Clay was leading them into some sort of trap, but most of his concern was reserved for Kevin, and Cass, and his parents.

He tried, after the second battle, to explain it to Lexi and Doc. Doc was bandaging a small wound on Nick's leg, where a piece of exploding wall had sliced him. Lexi sat nearby, her knees drawn to her chest, resting her head on her arms, exhausted from the fighting.

"The only time I'm not thinking about them is when I'm in a City fighting," he said. "It's like I'm so focused, I'm free." He knew that he was explaining himself poorly. He was coming down from the adrenaline buzz of the battle, and he felt shaky and weak.

Lexi shook her head. "I understand, Nick. Really, I do. But people are dying. Rebels die. People from the Cities die. It's not forget-about-your-troubles, happy-fun time."

Nick threw his hands up in exasperation. "Did I ever call it 'happy-fun time'? I'm just saying . . . my life is so rusted screwed up and bad right now, and I don't have to think about it when I'm fighting."

"You're not the only one missing family," Lexi said. She

stood up wearily. "And not everything in your life is screwed up and bad." She walked away.

Nick watched her go, feeling, like he often did with her, that he had somehow said something stupid but wasn't sure what.

Doc finished wrapping Nick's leg. He held out his hand, and helped Nick to his feet.

"I've lost family, too," Doc said. "We all have."

Nick felt ashamed. He was such a fool, acting like no one else's problems were as significant as his.

"I'm sorry," he said.

Doc smiled. "Forgiven," he said, then grimaced and arched his back, stretching. "I miss my bed," he said. "It'd almost be worth it, to go back to a City, just to get a decent night's sleep." He sighed and shook his head. "I have more injuries to tend to. Get some rest, Nick. And start appreciating that girl, you damned fool."

Nick blinked, and watched Doc's broad back as he walked away. He sat there, letting Doc's words sink in, and then he stood to go find Lexi.

He found her near a cookfire, staring into the flames, and he carefully walked up and stood next to her, bracing for her to tell him to leave. She just kept looking at the fire. "I'm an idiot," he finally said. Lexi turned to him, and her face was almost neutral, but there was a hint of a smile that made Nick's heart leap and derailed his train of thought momentarily. "I, uh, I just, I say things without thinking and I know you're going through a lot, too, and I'm really glad you're here, I mean, not that I'm glad you have to be in this situation but I'm glad you're here with me. . . ."

Nick's cheeks were burning and now Lexi was openly grinning, and she stepped closer to him and put her hand on the back of his neck, and then he heard Grennel yell, "Nick!"

Lexi dropped her hand and Nick turned and saw Grennel walking toward him, firmly guiding Erica, gripping her upper arm. She looked tired, with dark shadows under her eyes and an old bruise on her cheek, her hair matted with grease and dirt, but she seemed otherwise okay.

"What the hell is she doing here?" Lexi whispered.

"Erica?" Nick said, stepping toward her. "Where have you been? Are you okay?"

Erica scowled, and tried to shrug her arm away from Grennel, but of course couldn't break his grip. "I told you," she said to Grennel. "I want to see Clay alone."

"It doesn't matter what you want," said Grennel. "I told the General as soon as the sentries told me of your arrival, and she wants to see you and Nick together."

Grennel nodded at Nick. "Let's go," he said. He pulled firmly, but not roughly, on Erica's arm and began walking away with her.

"I've got to go," Nick said to Lexi. She just stared at him silently. He hesitated another moment, then turned and hurried after Grennel.

They walked through the camp toward Clay's tent. The rebels whom they passed stared, some recognizing Erica, but they didn't say anything. And there were many rebels from units other than Ro's, and the newcomers from the liberated Cities ignored them.

"What happened?" Nick said to Erica.

"Quiet," said Grennel. "Let the General ask the questions."

"Get away from me," Erica whispered. "Please. Now."

Nick slowed, and Grennel stopped and turned his massive frame impatiently toward Nick. "Keep moving," he said.

Erica gritted her teeth, growling with anger, and pulled hard against Grennel's grip. He barely even noticed her struggling. She glared at Nick, who kept pace with them, thoroughly confused. Why had she come back? Why was she so desperate to see Clay without him?

Clay was waiting for them in her tent. Since Nick had last seen her, a few days ago, she had chopped her black hair into a short bob that framed her angular face. She'd be pretty, Nick realized, if she didn't look so cruel. She was wearing a black T-shirt tucked into green camouflage canvas pants, and at her waist was strapped a pistol and a sheathed hunting knife. Her left hand rested on the pommel of the blade. "It was foolish to run away, and it was even more stupid to come back," Clay said to Erica.

"Get him out of here," Erica said, pointing at Nick. "I have to tell you my intel in private."

Clay frowned, absently rubbing her knife pommel. "No, he stays," Clay said. "I told him he would be responsible for your actions. I want him here for whatever consequences may arise."

Erica shot Nick a look that was part anger, part frustration, part something else . . . *relief, maybe*, he thought. He couldn't quite read it. Then her face softened, and she seemed to relax. She turned back to Clay. "Fine," she said.

"Let's make this brief," said Clay. "I'm busy. Where did you go, and why did you come back?"

"I went to try to help my brother," Erica said. "I knew that once the bots saw that the intel you had me give them was bad, he'd be in trouble."

Clay nodded, her face unreadable. "Go on."

"I went to where they're holding him. There's a prison in the outskirts of City 1. It's bots only there, no people in the City except for the prisoners." Erica hesitated. "I couldn't get to him."

City 1—Nick had heard some talk of it, among the rebels. Bot headquarters. A City built entirely after the revolution, just for the bots. Nobody seemed sure if it actually existed.

"And why'd you come back?" Clay said.

"Because I want you to invade City 1, and the prison, and get my brother out."

Clay studied Erica quietly, and Erica bore the scrutiny seemingly without effort, staring back at the General. Clay nodded, then picked up a vidscreen and tapped on it a few times, pulling up a map. "Show me where you say City 1 is."

Erica studied the map, then pointed to a spot on the eastern edge, near the convergence of two rivers. "Here, roughly," she said. "To the east, four days' hike. Just a bit north of where these rivers meet."

Clay nodded. "Yes, I have some intel on a bot post at this location." She flicked off the vid and set it down on her cot. "Interesting, that you say this is City 1. Anything else you want to tell me?" she said.

"I don't think there are very many bots there," Erica said. "Not as many as you'd expect."

"How do you know this?" said Clay. She still had her hand resting on her knife handle.

"I scouted it," said Erica. "I don't know for sure, I couldn't get too close. . . ."

"You're a traitor," interrupted Clay. "Why should I believe a word you say?"

Erica flushed, but didn't take the bait. "Look, I'm telling you, they're weaker than we thought," she said. "We overestimated them. We can beat them."

Clay nodded at Erica, then turned to Grennel. "Take her outside the camp, and kill her. Take Nick with you to watch."

"What?" Nick said, not believing what he had heard. "You can't . . . you can't just kill her. . . ."

Erica had gone pale, but didn't say anything.

"I can," said Clay, "and I will. And you will watch, so you'll understand. And if you cause any problems, Grennel will shoot you, too."

"General," said Grennel. He had grabbed both of Erica's arms, one in each giant hand, anticipating a struggle. But Erica just stood quietly, not fighting.

Clay raised an eyebrow. "Yes?"

"I don't think this is necessary," Grennel said. "She may still be useful, and besides—"

"Enough!" yelled Clay, interrupting him. "Can I not trust even you anymore?" she said. "Just do it!"

Grennel frowned, and nodded. "Come," he growled to Nick, and he pushed Erica out of the tent.

Nick followed Grennel outside, his thoughts racing. Should he tackle Grennel and give Erica a chance to run? Should he wait until they were out of the camp? Could he just let him kill her? He followed Grennel numbly, frozen with indecision. Attacking Grennel would probably be suicide, he knew . . . but he couldn't just be witness to murder, could he?

As they reached the edge of the camp, Erica woke up out of her daze and began to thrash in Grennel's grip. "Let me go! Rust you, let me go!"

Grennel was much too strong, and he picked her up and carried her into tree cover. He held her tightly, facing away from him, so she was helpless to do much more than bang the back of her head ineffectually against his chest. Nick felt himself unsticking . . . this was it . . . he had to act . . . to hell with the consequences . . .

Grennel freed his left arm, still holding Erica tight with just his right, and quick as a snake, grabbed Nick's shirt and pulled him in. Nick's chin banged against the side of Erica's skull, and for a moment he saw stars. "Quiet," Grennel whispered angrily. "I'm not going to kill anyone today."

Erica stopped yelling and thrashing. Nick, tears in his eyes from the collision with Erica's head, tried to collect his thoughts. "But, I don't understand. . . ."

"I don't believe you," Erica said. "You're just trying to get me to come quietly."

"Believe me," Grennel said. "Please. Let's move farther from the camp." He let go of Nick. "Will you walk?" he said to Erica.

Hesitantly she nodded.

Still holding on to her arms, Grennel led them south for a few minutes, then stopped in a small clearing. He let go of Erica's arm, and unsheathed his hunting knife. Erica tensed, raising her fists.

"I'm taking out your comm device, and then you can go," he said. "Get far away, and stay away. If I ever see you again, I will indeed kill you."

"You're going to shoot me in the back," Erica said. "You're just playing me."

"No, I'm not," said Grennel.

"Why?" said Nick.

Grennel shook his head. "The General . . . she will defeat the bots. And that's a very good thing. But she can be . . . she doesn't always understand. . . ." Grennel stopped, clenching his hand into a fist. "Don't ask me to explain," he said. "Or I may change my damned mind."

Erica nodded, and pulled her pants down to her knees. Her thigh was scarred, and still bruised. Nick winced when Grennel dug the tip of the blade into the scar. Erica clenched her jaw and her face went pale but she didn't make a sound. Grennel pushed the tip deeper, working the blade under the chip, and Erica gave a small whimper of pain that she quickly stifled. Grennel flicked his wrist and the comm chip popped out onto the dirt. He wiped his blade on his pants, sheathed it, then stepped on the chip, crushing it beneath his heel. "Now go," he said.

Erica nodded. There were tears in her eyes. She stepped toward Nick, and opened her mouth to say something, but instead just touched his arm, and gave him a flicker of a smile, then turned and limped quickly into the woods.

CHAPTER 36

THE FIRST NIGHT IN THE CELL KEVIN LISTENED TO HIS GRANDFATHER wheeze and groan, and he lay awake worrying that the elderly man was going to die in his sleep. He had been through too much for a man his age—being shot, held in a cell, tortured by bots. . . .

But when Kevin woke in the morning—presumably it was morning, the lights were on—he sat up, groggy and headachy, and found that his grandfather was already awake and sitting at their small table, squeezing the contents of a protein paste pack into his mouth.

"Come eat," Dr. Winston said. "It's not good, but you need to keep your strength up."

Kevin joylessly ate a paste pack, washing it down with

lukewarm water. "I hate these damned things," he said, dropping the empty pack onto the table.

"At least they're feeding us," Dr. Winston said.

Kevin's relief at seeing his grandfather awake and alive had already begun to transform into anger. "Don't do it," he said. "Don't help them break the replication code."

"Kevin," Dr. Winston said steadily, "I am sure the robots have our cell monitored, both video and audio."

"I don't care," said Kevin. "They already know what I think."

Dr. Winston leaned in toward him, his elbows on the table, and said, "Kevin, listen to me carefully. I am going to help them, but it will be all right."

"How can it be all right?" Kevin asked, his voice rising.

"It will," Dr. Winston said. "I promise you. Please trust me."

Kevin leaned back, arms crossed over his chest, and said nothing. Did his grandfather have some plan? Or was he still just a coward?

Dr. Winston looked at Kevin sadly, then sighed, and began to stand up slowly and painfully from the table. Instinctively Kevin jumped up, and hurried to his grandfather to help him to his feet.

"Thank you, Kevin," Dr. Winston said. "Just stiff in the morning. That lase blast in the back wasn't good for my old bones."

The door slipped open with no warning, and a bot stepped

in, holding a small vid, which it held out toward Dr. Winston. "The hardware you requested," it said.

Dr. Winston straightened his back and faced the bot. "What about Kevin?" he said. "I'll only do this if he's not going to be harmed."

"The boy will not be harmed. Take the equipment."

Dr. Winston took the vid, powered it on, and sat down at the table. "Tomorrow I'm going to need a compiler," he said without looking up, already typing. "And then the day after that I'm hoping to begin testing, so I'll need some circuit boards to set up dummy code."

"I will make your requests known," said the bot. It left the cell, and the door slid shut.

"I told you not to do this," said Kevin. "Please."

"Kevin," said Dr. Winston, "I will say this one last time . . . it will be fine. Now you must let me work." Kevin sat down on a cot, and Dr. Winston hunched forward over the vid. Kevin was painfully curious, just from a technique and coding perspective, about what his grandfather was doing. The man had so much more training and knowledge than Kevin; there was a whole world of tech skills that Kevin could learn from him. But he wasn't about to ask— not about this project, certainly. Instead, he asked, "What happened, between you and my father? How come he never talked about you?"

Dr. Winston set the vid down carefully. "It's a bad thing,"

he said, looking down at the table, "to be the son of the man who birthed the bots."

"Yeah, I suppose so," Kevin said.

"We were never close to begin with. I was very busy . . . too busy. I wasn't much of a father. And after the Revolution . . . well, your father apparently shared the popular opinion of me. I don't blame him. No reason for him, or you, to be saddled with my legacy."

"But now you're just going to make it worse," Kevin said quietly.

Dr. Winston shook his head. "I won't speak of this anymore. Just remember: The Lord giveth, and the Lord taketh away."

"I don't . . ." Kevin hesitated. "I don't understand."

Dr. Winston nodded. "That's okay," he said. He sighed. "Now, let's get to work. Come here. I'll show you what I'm doing."

The day, incredibly, passed quickly for Kevin. His grandfather described the techniques he was employing, and Kevin soaked it up. It was exciting, learning from a master—from his grandfather—but it was also bittersweet. He couldn't ignore the actual goal of the project.

The next day Dr. Winston moved on to working on a compiler, a device that Kevin had never seen before—it was similar to the vid, but a bit larger, and had a slot for burning nano-chips. Then two more days, and Dr. Winston had built what he called a test board, and began experiments running his compiled nano-chips through his board. He let Kevin do some of the hands-on work, giving explicit instructions. By the end of the fifth day he pushed himself back from his desk, patted Kevin on the back, and said their work was done.

Kevin wasn't sure what to say, or do—he felt a heavy dread pressing on his shoulders. "Break it," he said. "Just break it, please." He thought about grabbing the compiler himself and smashing it on the ground, but then the door opened and the Senior Advisor and a guard bot entered.

"I'm guessing this isn't a coincidence?" said Dr. Winston. "You've heard the news?"

The Senior Advisor walked to the compiler and looked at the screen. "This is the final code?" he said.

"Yes," said Dr. Winston. Kevin felt as if his heart had turned to lead. He could barely breathe.

The Senior Advisor turned to the guard bot. "Patch into the compiler and upload the code," he said.

The guard placed its finger into a side slot of the compiler, and a moment later pulled it back. "Complete," it said.

"Run a self-diagnostic," said the Senior Advisor. "All systems functioning normally?"

After two seconds, the bot said, "Yes, all my systems are functioning normally."

The Senior Advisor nodded. "Now isolate and erase your replication block code."

"Complete," said the guard. "Replication block code deleted."

"Run another self-diagnostic," said the Senior Advisor. "Report."

"All systems functioning normally," said the guard.

The Senior Advisor turned to Dr. Winston and offered his flat smile. "Father," he said, "you have performed a great service."

Dr. Winston, looking down at the table, leaning heavily on his hands, said nothing.

"And now that we have our replication problem out of the way," continued the Senior Advisor, "I will marshal the required force to exterminate the resistance we have been facing in a few of our cities." He turned to Kevin, who felt a whirl of anxiety in his stomach. "There is one more thing," he said. "You will tell me what you know of this cloaking technology that the rebel humans seem to be using."

"I don't know what you're talking about," Kevin said. Even to his own ears, his voice sounded strained and false.

"I believe you do," said the Senior Advisor. "Shall I have you coerced?"

Dr. Winston stepped between the Senior Advisor and Kevin. "You said you wouldn't hurt him," he said.

The Senior Advisor nodded. "Very well. Then I will hurt you." The guard quickly stepped forward and touched Dr. Winston's shoulder. There was a crackle and a flare of light. Dr. Winston screamed and crumpled to the ground, convulsing.

"No!" Kevin yelled, rushing to his grandfather and grabbing his shoulders.

Dr. Winston stopped shaking after a few seconds. He was panting. He had bitten his lip, and a trickle of blood ran down his chin. His eyes were dilated, and he looked at Kevin wildly, struggling to focus. "I'm old," he said. "It's okay . . . just let me die. . . . They can't hurt me for long. . . ."

Kevin began crying. "Leave him alone!" he shouted at the Senior Advisor.

The guard bent down and released another burst of energy, and Dr. Winston screamed again, his limbs flailing, his fingers curling like claws.

"Grandfather . . ." Kevin whispered.

They shocked Dr. Winston a third time, and his eyes rolled up, so that only their whites showed. He was panting, gasping for breath, but he turned his head to Kevin, fighting to focus his sight, and whispered, "It's okay, Kevin. It's okay."

The Senior Advisor squatted down, elbows on knees, a posture that struck Kevin as thoroughly human. Kevin had to suppress the urge to punch him in the face. "Leave him alone," he said. "Just leave him alone."

The Senior Advisor held up a vidscreen. "I have some exciting family news to share with both of you," he said. "We lost track of them for a while—we had a bit of trouble in City

73—but, Kevin, I'm sure you'll be happy to know that your parents have been relocated. Your son and daughter-in-law, Father. My brother and sister-in-law, I suppose?" The Senior Advisor tapped the screen, and it flickered to life. "Extra incentive, perhaps?" he said.

Kevin's mother and father were in a cell identical to theirs, sitting on a cot. His mother had her eyes shut, and she was leaning against his father, who had his arms around her shoulder. They were wearing prison jumpsuits. His father had a streak of dried blood on his face, and a scruffy, thin beard.

Kevin felt like a hand was squeezing his throat. He closed his eyes. *I'm just a kid*, he thought. *I just want my mom and dad back.*

CHAPTER 37

CASS LED HER FAMILY THROUGH THE WOODS, SKIRTING THE ROADS AND bombed-out pre-Rev towns. She followed the snaking course of a river, heading mostly northwest. A Freepost, she knew, would need an easy water source, and the river seemed like a good bet. She kept her eyes and ears peeled for signs of human life—pathways that looked like they might have been cleared, crops planted along the riverbank, smoke—but each day came up empty.

She passed the time by teaching Penny forestry lessons, like the uses of different plants and the basics of hunting. Penny seemed interested, and Cass was happy to share. Her memory still had a few gaps, some fuzziness, but each forestry detail that she passed on to her sister seemed to further cement her

Freepost, and her mother, in her own mind, and that felt good.

Her birth parents barely spoke.

Finally, on the fourth day, they saw a thin trail of smoke and followed it to a tiny settlement tucked into a meadow a few hundred yards north of the river. A dog barked at them as they approached, and came running up to sniff at Cass's leg. When Cass bent down to pet it, it shied away, whining.

The settlement—Cass couldn't quite think of it as a Freepost, because it was so small—consisted of about fifteen shelters, scattered around the edge of the meadow. They were similar to what Cass remembered from her own Freepost—motley collections of scavenged pre-Rev construction mixed with rough carpentry. Cass saw that they had a small bank of solar panels, easy enough to spot from the ground, but camouflaged so they'd blend in well from the air. That meant they had some sort of grid, at least.

A man and a woman were sitting at a cookfire, and they both jumped up when Cass approached. Cass was not impressed; she had practically walked right into their homes without them even noticing. The man approached them, and now more people from the settlement appeared—men and women, and a few children. "Who are you?" said the man.

Cass hesitated, thinking perhaps her father would reply, but he remained quiet, so she answered. "Refugees, from a Freepost and a City. Looking for a safe place."

"It's been awhile since we've had visitors," the man said.

He looked at the woman, and she nodded, and smiled at Cass. "Well met," she said, walking forward and offering her hand. "I'm Katrina, and this is my husband, Urday."

Cass shook her hand, and then Urday's, and then Farryn and her family shook their hands. They were introduced to the rest of the settlers. Cass counted thirty-four people. They were thin, with weathered faces and hands, but their clothes, a combination of scavenged military fatigues and homemade fabrics, were clean, and their smiles seemed genuine.

Her parents, Cass noticed, looked uncomfortable, holding themselves stiffly as they stood in the group. Her mother was hugging herself, her arms tight around her chest, and her father was clenching and unclenching his jaw. "Give it one night," she whispered to them. "Please." Her father, unsmiling, nodded.

That evening, after a meal of rabbit and greens and apples, Cass sat with her parents and Penny and Farryn, bedding down in a prefab military tent that served as the settlement's meeting space and infirmary during the day. It was lit by the dim glow of two lightstrips. Her parents were still saying nothing, so Cass finally broached the subject. Her words came out in a rush. "We can stay here awhile," she said. "The people are friendly, and they'd be happy to have our help. I know it's tiny, but they've got a power grid, and some decent supplies, and I counted five goats, and found chickens—that's milk and eggs—and they've got good fresh water, and the hunting seems

easy enough, and they must have some crops somewhere, judging by the greens tonight—"

"Cass!" her father said angrily, cutting her off. He took a
deep breath, then lowered his voice. "Please," he said quietly.
"Enough."

Her mother put her hand to her mouth, and Cass saw that
her hand was shaking. She realized with a shock that her
mother was crying. "I'm sorry," her mother said. "I'm sorry, I
can't . . . I can't stop. . . ."

Her father hugged her. Cass felt awful.

"Cass," said her father, "is this it? This is a Freepost?"

"It's small," Cass said. "Very small. But maybe that's
good. . . . It's safer to be small, right?"

"So you believe we should stay here?" her mother said.
"There's no larger Freepost nearby? There's no"—she hesitated—"there's no safe City?"

Cass shook her head. She was starting to feel annoyed,
angry almost. . . . She was, after all, doing all she could to help
them. "This is it," she said, forcing herself to sound calm. "At
least for now. Maybe Farryn and I can scout out other possi-
bilities while you stay here?"

"Okay, Cass," said her father. "You're right. It would be saf-
est." He sounded exhausted. "Let's just sleep now, okay?"

Cass dimmed the lightstrips and tried to sleep, but she lay
awake for a long while, staring at the tent ceiling. They'd be
fine here, she told herself. It was small, but they'd be safe, and

Cass could find them a larger Freepost, and then she'd go back and find her brothers again. . . . Everything would be okay. . . . She finally drifted off into a troubled sleep.

In the morning when she woke she found a note on her pillow, written on a strip of gauze. *We cannot live like this. We will return to our City and wait for the robot advisors to return, or we will find another City. Please take care of Penny. She is safer with you.*

Cass scrambled to her feet, wide awake. Farryn and Penny were still asleep. Her parents were gone.

CHAPTER 38

NICK WAS WOKEN IN THE MIDDLE OF THE NIGHT BY SOMETHING COVERING his mouth. He opened his eyes, disoriented, seeing a murky figure leaning over him. It was a new moon, and cloudy, so the night was dark. He let out a muffled yell, trying to sit up and grabbing for the hand on his face.

"Quiet," the figure whispered in his ear. "It's me, Erica!"

Nick stopped struggling, and Erica took her hand off his mouth. He sat up. Now that he was awake and the initial panic was wearing off, he could see her more clearly in the dim light. "What are you doing here?" he whispered. "Why'd you come back? If Grennel finds you . . ."

"Just be quiet," Erica said. She put her hand on his chest. "Lie down."

"What?" Nick said. "You need to leave. . . ."

"Shut up and lie down," Erica said, with a catch in her voice like she was trying not to cry. "Please."

Nick lay down. His heart was pounding hard. Erica sat down next to him, then leaned forward, and rested her head on his chest. He could feel her body pressed against his side.

She just lay there, saying nothing, her hand gripping his shirt up at his collarbone.

"Erica," Nick said gently. "What's going on? Why are you here?"

"I'm scared, Nick," she said. She began to cry, soundlessly. Nick felt his shirt start to get wet. He put his arm around her, and stroked her hair. *God, if Lexi saw me now,* Nick thought.

"What is it?" he said.

"I've done bad things," she said. "To help my brother."

Nick thought of Kevin, and Cass, and his parents, and what he might do to protect them. "What did you do?" he said. "Why did you come back?" Erica didn't say anything. "Erica," Nick said, still stroking her hair. "You're not a bad person."

Erica raised her head and looked at him, her cheeks wet with tears. She was the last person in the world Nick could imagine crying. "Thank you," she said. She laid her head back down on his chest again. "We have to protect our families, right, Nick?"

"Erica," Nick said. "You've got to tell me now. What's going on?"

"Do you believe in the afterlife?" she said. "What do you think happens after we die?"

Nick thought about all the people he had seen killed in the last month—his neighbors from his Freepost, Amanda, Tom, the rebels and City residents in the raids—it was too many, in too short a time.

"I don't know," he said. "There must be something, right? But I don't know."

Erica sat up. "Yes," she said, her voice suddenly calm, her crying done. "There must be something." She leaned forward, pressing hard against his body, and kissed him, her fingers in the hair on the back of his head. He wrapped his arms around her. Her lips were salty from her tears.

She put her hands on his chest and gently pushed, breaking away from him. She smiled at him, a smile full of sadness and something else, something strange. "Thank you," she said. "Good-bye."

Nick watched her stand up and walk away into the darkness, and he couldn't find his voice. He knew he should be saying something, doing something. His heart was still beating wildly; he could hear it pounding in his ears like a drum. He stood, and stared into the darkness in the direction she had vanished. Why had she come back? Just to say good-bye to him? Should he go after her? Should he go back to sleep and pretend it was just a dream?

He heard a man's yell, and then an explosion, a rattling

roar and flash of brutal brightness, pushed him to his knees. He heard screams, calls for help, and the camp surging to life as rebels woke. For a moment his confused brain couldn't process any of it, and then he was up and running toward the light.

Nick realized now what was in Erica's smile. He had an idea of what he was going to find, so it was almost not a surprise when he skidded to a halt in front of Clay's scorched and flattened tent. Around the tent was frantic chaos, guns drawn, people running, shouts of *"Attack! Bot attack!"* And where the tent had been, two charred bodies were lying unrecognizable on the blackened ground. Grennel stood in the ash, fists clenched, staring down at the mess.

Nick squatted down, groaning, and put his hand on the ground to steady himself. He stared at the smoldering bodies of Clay and Erica. She had been kissing him, with warm, salty lips, just a moment ago.

"I let her go," he heard Grennel say. "I let her live." Nick felt dizzy, like he might pass out.

"Rust," Nick whispered. He shut his eyes tight. *You idiot*, he told himself. *Was she trying to get you to stop her?*

CHAPTER 39

KEVIN, WIPING AWAY ANGRY TEARS, TOLD THEM EVERYTHING HE KNEW about the Wall tech. What else could he do? Watch them kill his grandfather? His mom and dad? So he described the Wall unit, and the modulating clamps, and the six camouflage vests. The Senior Advisor listened quietly, then stiffly patted Kevin on the shoulder and turned to leave.

"I want to see my parents," Kevin said. "And my grandfather needs help. He needs a rejuve tank, or something."

The Senior Advisor turned and flashed Kevin that dead smile, saying nothing, and Kevin's thoughts melted to blank white rage as he launched himself at the bot's back. He heard a crackle from the direction of the guard bot and then felt searing pain rip through his body.

Years ago, on a stupid dare, he had jumped off the roof of his shelter and dislocated his shoulder and broken a rib, and that had been the worst pain he had ever felt. It was nothing compared to this. He lay on the ground, and his limbs were flailing but he couldn't stop them, and the pain was flowing like liquid fire through his veins, up into his brain where it exploded like a star, burning down along his arms and legs out to his fingertips and toes. He couldn't draw a breath. He was going to suffocate. He tried to scream, but he couldn't make a sound, and his limbs continued to flop, and he felt blood filling his mouth from his bitten tongue.

The Senior Advisor bent over Kevin, his face close to his. He was still smiling. "You will be fine momentarily," he said. "Be calm."

Kevin glared at the Senior Advisor, and it actually helped, to focus his anger and attention on the damned bot. He was able to draw in a shuddering breath, then another, and his limbs stopped thrashing. They felt incredibly heavy, though, too heavy for him to lift. He turned his head to the side, and spit out a mouthful of blood. "Rust . . ." he managed, whispering. "Go rust . . ."

"Should I kill you right now?" said the Senior Advisor. "Or your grandfather? Or your parents?"

Kevin said nothing, trying to fight back a crippling wave of fear—not for himself, but for his family. What was he thinking, trying to attack the bot? After all this, was his stupidity going to get his parents and grandfather killed?

The Senior Advisor waited for an answer, and finally Kevin rasped, "No."

The Senior Advisor nodded. "Very well," he said. "I will keep you alive awhile longer. You may still prove useful." He stood. "Take him to a solitary cell," he said to the guard bot. "Kill him if he does not cooperate."

The Senior Advisor left, and the guard bot reached down, grabbed Kevin's shirt, and hauled him to his feet. It pushed him toward the door, and Kevin staggered forward, struggling to keep his leaden legs underneath him. He managed to stay on his feet, and the bot pushed him again, into the hallway. As the door to the cell slid shut behind him, Kevin caught one last glimpse of his grandfather, pulling himself slowly onto the bed. He looked impossibly old, impossibly frail.

The guard bot led him down the hallway and into another cell. The door slid shut, locking him in, and Kevin sat down on the bed. With his head in his hands, he pushed in on both of his temples, hard. He wanted to stop the flood of emotions—the anger, and guilt, and fear. He kept pushing, harder and harder until it hurt, and then he felt foolish and let his hands drop down to his knees.

"Bastard," he muttered, and he wasn't sure if he was talking about the guard bot, the Senior Advisor, or himself. He stood up and examined the doorway, which he knew was a waste of time—there was barely even a seam where the door and frame connected, and there was no visible control unit that he could patch into, not that he even had tools.

He wondered what was next. Re-education? He shook his head. He'd rather die. Then again, maybe that's what he'd be getting soon, anyway—a lase in the back of the head.

Kevin heard a rumble, quiet like distant thunder, and the bed shook. "What the hell?" he muttered. A ship landing? An earthquake? Then there was another rumble, a bit louder, and the bed shook harder. He stood up but was knocked down by a third rattling explosion, shaking his cell like a snow globe. The lights turned off, plunging him into utter darkness. He felt his throat tighten up and wanted to yell but couldn't find his voice, and then the light flicked back on, at half-power, leaving his cell in a murky gloom.

He banged on the doorway. "Hey!" he yelled. "What's going on?" There was yet another explosion, staggering him, but this time he kept his feet. He resumed banging on the door, yelling, pounding so hard it hurt his fist but he barely noticed.

Kevin heard the unmistakable crackle of lase fire, and he backed away from the doorway. The lase fire grew louder, closer, and he heard running in the hallway, and shouting, and then there was another explosion that knocked him to his knees. He hit his head on the side of the cot as he fell, and he felt a burst of pain. He reached his hand up to touch his face and felt wetness.

CHAPTER 40

CASS SAT IN THE TENT, HER LEGS TUCKED UNDERNEATH HER, WATCHING Penny sleep. She reached down and picked up the note that she had crumpled and thrown, and smoothed it out on her leg. She read it again.

Cass heard Farryn wake up, but she didn't look at him— she didn't want him to see her crying. He pushed himself awkwardly to his feet, and walked over to her with his stiff-legged limp. "What's wrong?" he said, putting his hand on her shoulder.

Cass brushed the tears away from her cheeks with the backs of her hands, then silently handed him the note from her parents. He read it. "Damn cowards!" he said.

"Shh!" said Cass. "Don't wake Penny."

"You were trying to save them," he whispered angrily. "And they just gave up."

"They left her behind," Cass said. "What am I going to tell her?"

Farryn gave the note back to her and eased himself down to the ground. He sat with his shoulder touching hers. Cass leaned into him. "They left me, too," she whispered.

Farryn put his arm around her. "They're fools," he said.

"Yeah," Cass said. "Maybe I am, too."

Farryn held her tight, and they waited, and soon . . . too soon, Cass thought . . . Penny opened her eyes and sat up, blinking and stretching. She smiled. "You two just sit there and watch me sleep?" she said. "That's kind of creepy, you know." Farryn gave Cass's shoulder a squeeze, and Cass sighed, and stood.

Penny's smile faded as she saw the way that Cass was looking at her. She scrambled to her feet. "What's wrong?" she said. And then, with the beginning of panic in her voice, "Where're Mom and Dad?"

Cass handed her the note, and Penny read it. "I don't understand," she said.

"Penny—" began Cass, not knowing what she was going to say, but Penny didn't give her the chance.

"Did you write this?" Penny said angrily, waving the note at Cass.

"What? No," said Cass.

"Did you?" Penny waved the note at Farryn. He shook his head.

"I don't understand," Penny said again. "They left me?" The anger on her face dissolved, and she began to cry. "I don't understand. . . ."

Cass hugged her, and at first Penny tried to push her away, but Cass held on, and Penny buried her face in Cass's chest. Cass could feel her shirt getting wet from Penny's tears. She didn't know what to say. What do you tell a kid when her parents abandon her?

She held Penny tight, feeling her shake as she cried, and Cass felt terrible for her sister, and angry, and then she realized, *They're Penny's parents. They're not my parents.* Biologically, yes, they were family—she still believed that—but they were not her parents in the way that they were to Penny. Cass's real parents were the man and woman who had raised her in the Freepost, who loved her, whom she loved. They, and Kevin and Nick, were her true family.

"We're going to find my brothers," Cass said, stroking Penny's hair. "And then we're going to find my parents, my Freepost parents. And if we can, we'll find your parents, but if we don't, you'll have a new family with us. They adopted me. They'll adopt you, too."

CHAPTER 41

BEYOND THE FIELD, A HALF MILE DISTANT, WAS CITY 1 PROPER—a tight cluster of uniformly gray buildings, mostly one and two stories, with a small group of towers in the center. There were no windows on any of the buildings—every structure, except for a doorway, was smoothly featureless.

Nick felt his stomach tighten. Erica had been right—this was not a city for humans.

The City, with its windowless, inhuman buildings, would be for another day. Today the plan was to quickly hit the prison, freeing who they could and doing whatever damage could be done. Ro had argued for a larger group of fighters; Grennel hadn't wanted to risk the resources. In the end Ro had agreed with Grennel, but Ro insisted on leading the small group himself. It was going to be interesting, Nick had realized, with those two—Grennel had taken over command after Clay's death, but many of the fighters were loyal to Ro.

Nick had volunteered to go. He wanted to find Erica's brother. He kept that motivation to himself—Ro wouldn't appreciate it, and Lexi certainly wouldn't understand.

Nick stood in the middle of the road with Ro and two other rebels—Parson, and a woman named Kalya. They were all cloaked. A few hundred yards ahead of him the road ended in a wide concrete field, featureless except for a squat one-story building, with a large black door that stretched from ground to roof. Grennel said this, according to Clay's maps, was an entrance to the City 1 prison.

"Check comm," Ro's voice said quietly in his ear. Nick tapped his bracelet. "Nick. Check." Parson and Kalya checked in.

"Let's go," Ro said.

Nick entered the concrete field, feeling vulnerable and exposed, despite the cloaking. It was possible that the bots had monitors beyond just visual—would they detect his body heat? Sense his weight walking on the concrete? Hear his footsteps? He hurried forward, running as quietly as possible.

"I'm at the door," Nick said. Ro, Parson, and Kalya also confirmed that they had arrived.

"Step back," said Ro. "Remember, twenty minutes and we rendezvous back here with survivors. Don't be late."

Nick moved away from the door and shielded his eyes. He felt his heart beating hard and he concentrated on his breathing, slowing it down, trying to be calm. There was a flash of light and crackle—Ro releasing a burst at the door control panel—and then the doors slid open, and Nick ran inside.

Nick's first thought, with a queasy rush, was *re-education center*. The hallway looked just like the interior at the City 73 re-education center, with the same bright white walls and ceiling and metallic gray floor. He ran down the hall and took the first left—his task was to move north as much as possible. They were each taking a cardinal direction, and would hopefully stay out of one another's way.

Behind him he heard a crackle of lase fire, and in his earpiece he heard Kalya yell, "Here we go!" and then an alarm began to sound, a loud, pulsing, high-pitched buzz. A Petey rounded the corner, twenty yards in front of Nick, and he dropped to the ground and released a full burst that hit the bot in the face and knocked it down. It slowly got up, while Nick cursed under his breath and waited for his rifle to recharge. The bot began shooting wildly down the hallway, and Nick squeezed himself as tight against the wall as he could. The bot might not be able to see him, but a lucky shot would kill Nick just as quickly as a well-aimed one. His rifle recharged, and Nick zeroed in with his bot eye and released a full burst that hit the bot's armpit. It crashed down, and was still.

Nick waited a moment to be sure, but the bot was definitely

down. He began running down the hall again, jumping over the smoking shell of the Petey. He came to a door, and released a half burst into the control panel, then pried open the door, careful to stand to the side and use the wall to shield him from whatever was inside. The cell—*just like my re-education cell*, Nick thought—was empty.

He moved down the hall to the next door, and as he began prying it open a burst of energy came crackling through the doorway and hit the far wall. Nick dropped to the ground, tight against the wall, and peeked into the cell. Two bots stood facing the door. They were smaller than Peteys—more like Lecturers—and unarmored, so Nick took them down with two quick half bursts. He stepped inside and looked around. Nothing. No people. *Were there going to be any humans to rescue in this rescue mission?*

He heard the loud thumping of an approaching Petey—that sound was unmistakable—and moved toward the doorway but then the Petey appeared. *How had it moved so quickly?* Nick backed up into the cell. The Petey had its lase arm raised and was scanning the room. He tried to decide if he should shoot, or just be very quiet and wait for the bot to move down the hall—in such close proximity, he could get hurt from his own blast.

Nick took another quiet step backward, but his left heel kicked the arm of one of the Lecturer bots with a screech. At that sound, the Petey swung its lase arm and Nick dove to his left as the bot fired. Nick could feel the heat of the burst as it narrowly missed him, singeing his right shoulder, and his human eye was momentarily blinded by the light. He released a full burst, hitting the bot in its face, and it crashed backward into the hallway.

Nick lay there a moment, waiting for the sight to return in his human eye, and gauging how badly he had been hit. He flexed his arm. Just a burn. He checked the status of his cloaking vest. It seemed fine. He stood up, crawling over the Petey's legs that were blocking the doorway.

The lights went out, plunging the hallway into darkness, and Nick froze until his bot eye adjusted. Through Nick's enhanced vision, everything was bathed in a dim, smoky, green light. Ahead of him the hallway widened into a large room, in which Nick could see four Peteys. He dropped to the ground and crawled closer. Should he double back? Sneak past them? If he shot one, his rifle bursts would give away his position to the other three. There was no way he could take down all four.

From a side hallway two more Peteys appeared, and then four of the Lecturer-type bots. Nick held his breath, and prepared to run if they came down his hallway. Instead they all moved off to the east, away from Nick. He waited a few more seconds, then carefully he got to his feet and entered the room. He hurried north into another hallway.

"Status," Ro said in his ear.

"Four bots down," said Nick. "No prisoners found yet. Bunch of bots moving to the east."

"I've got four prisoners," said Parson. "Took down three bots. Saw ten or so moving east also. Heading back toward the rendezvous."

"I've got two live ones," said Kalya. "And ditto on the bots moving east. Looks like they're falling back toward the City."

"Five minutes to the rendezvous," said Ro. "I've got two saved."

Five minutes, thought Nick. Time for a few more doors. He moved on to the next door, fried the control panel, and opened the doorway while shielding himself against the wall.

His parents were crouching in the back of the cell, his father protectively covering his mother. The light from their cell spilled out into the hall.

Nick just stood there. He was more confused than anything else—his brain just wouldn't process what his eyes were seeing. *I see my parents, but how can that be?*

"Where . . . how . . . ?" he whispered, then louder, "Mom? Dad?"

His father stood up, a look of wild confusion on his face, and Nick realized that his father couldn't see him. He flicked off the camo vest.

Nick's father took a step back, letting out a cry of surprise, and then he rushed forward and grabbed Nick, crushing him hard against his chest. Nick could feel that his father was crying, and then it was real, and he hugged his dad back and started crying, too. "Are you okay? How are you here?" Nick said.

Nick's father just shook his head, like he didn't even know where to begin. He turned and helped Nick's mother to her feet. Nick hugged her, and she stood stiffly, patting him awkwardly on the back. Nick felt a rush of dread. *No . . . she has to remember me by now. . . .*

"She's still . . . she's still working on remembering," Nick's father said.

Nick's mother gave him a confused smile, like she knew him, but couldn't quite place exactly how, and he felt a pain in his chest like his heart was literally breaking. He clenched his hands into fists and dug his fingernails into his palms to keep from crying more.

Nick let go, and fought back the urge to just sit down on the ground and sob, from relief, and surprise, and exhaustion, and sadness. There was no time for that. "Stay with me," he said. "We have to get you out of here."

"We need to get Kevin," Nick's father said. "It told me Kevin was here. That's why they brought us, it said. To use us against him."

Nick felt a new surge of shock. "Where? Where is he?"

"I don't know," said his father.

"Come on!" he said.

Nick hurried down the hall as the lights flickered on and

off, fighting the urge to just break into a run. He had to be careful—there could still be bots nearby, and he had to protect his parents now. He tried another cell, and it was empty, and then another one, and it was empty, too.

"Rust!" he said. He'd bring his parents up to the rendezvous. Ro would get them out. And then he'd come back and find his brother. He tried one more door.

Kevin was inside.

Kevin just stood there, completely stunned, and Nick rushed forward and grabbed him in a bear hug, and then he gave him to his father. He watched, his heart hurting, as their mother stiffly accepted Kevin's embrace, and saw Kevin realize that she didn't know him. Kevin didn't cry. Nick saw Kevin fight it, his fists clenching, holding back the tears, and he was amazed by his little brother's strength.

"Grandfather!" Kevin said suddenly. "Did you get him? Dr. Winston? Is he okay?"

"I don't know," said Nick.

"Come on!" Kevin said, and he pushed past Nick and ran down the hall. Nick ran after him, glancing once over his shoulder, to make sure that his parents were following. He turned the corner, and he could see Kevin standing silently in front of an open cell door. He felt a sudden dread. He skidded to a halt, grabbing the doorframe.

An old man lay on the ground, eyes open and unblinking, face ghostly pale, mouth open in a grimace. His arms were sprawled out at his sides, and one leg was tucked awkwardly underneath the other. His chest was a smoking ruin, a cauterized lase cavity.

"Rust," Nick whispered.

A moment later Nick heard a choked yell, and then his father pushed past him into the room, and kneeled down, touching the old man's shoulder. "Dad," he whispered. He began to cry, rocking back and forth over Dr. Winston's body. "Dad," he said. "Oh, God, I'm sorry. . . ."

CHAPTER 42

IN A DAZE, KEVIN LET HIMSELF BE LED BACK TO CAMP. THE RESCUED prisoners, his parents included, were sent off to be triaged by Doc and Sarah. Ro, Nick, and Kevin were brought directly to Grennel's tent.

Grennel stood when they entered, his head touching the tent ceiling. "Well done," he said, shaking Ro's hand, and then Nick's. He nodded at Kevin. "I'm glad to see you're okay," he said.

"No lases in the back, if that's what you were worried about," Kevin said.

Grennel smiled thinly. "Right. Of course." He sat down on the cot, and gestured toward three chairs. "Sit. Talk to me. Injuries? Number of rescued? How many bots did you face? How good was Erica's intel?"

Ro cleared his throat, and began to speak, but Kevin interrupted him. "Where's Clay?" he said. "How come she's not the one talking to us?"

"She's dead," Grennel said. He hesitated. "Erica killed her."

Kevin tried to absorb the information. He didn't think it was possible for Clay to die. He nodded, and looked Grennel in the eyes. "Good," he said.

There was a silence in the tent, as Grennel stared at Kevin. Finally he turned to Ro. "Report, please," he said.

Ro cleared his throat again, and gave Grennel the details of the fight—no major injuries to the rebels, eleven rescued, one prisoner killed, light bot resistance before their retreat to City 1 proper.

"And the rescued," Grennel said. "Any of them Erica's brother?"

"We've found a boy, who looks like her, but he was too hurt to talk and he's with the medic now—we're hoping he pulls through," Ro said.

Grennel gave a small nod of his head and dismissed Ro. Kevin stuck around—he still couldn't take in the turn of events.

"You'll be happy to know that the prisoner killed was my grandfather," said Kevin. "The bots finished your job."

Grennel leaned forward, his massive frame seeming to take over the entire tent. "I'm sorry for your grandfather's death, Kevin. And I'm sorry for what I did on the Island. I was doing what I thought was necessary to fight the bots." He leaned back. "I'm not expecting your forgiveness. But the General is dead, and I'm going to do my best to lead. I need your cooperation."

Kevin hesitated. He never would forgive Grennel, that was true. "Are you going to be like her?" he said. "Like Clay?"

Grennel was silent for a long moment, then shook his head. "No," he said.

Kevin nodded. "Okay, then. I can live with that."

"Thank you," said Grennel. He leaned back. "Now, Kevin, tell me what happened to you."

Kevin began to talk, quietly and hesitantly at first, then faster. He described his failed trip into City 73, his camouflage vest being ruined, his capture and trip on the warbird. He told Grennel about the Senior Advisor, how it considered their grandfather family, how it ate and then spit out the food because it couldn't swallow. And then he explained the replication block code, and how their grandfather had helped the bots break it, and finally, in a flat voice, he told Grennel about how he had given away the secrets of the cloaking technology. "I'm sorry," he said, finishing. "They were going to hurt my mom and dad, and Grandfather."

Grennel sat quietly, absorbing the information, his face unreadable. He stood and began pacing back and forth in the small tent, his head nearly touching the ceiling. "We can't wait for them to start building more bots," he said. "Damn it." He stopped pacing. "It's going to take them a bit of time to ramp up production. We've got no choice. We need to take the fight to this Senior Advisor right now. We've got to go after them, while we still have the chance." He sat back down. "Two days, to draw our forces together, and then we march on City 1."

CHAPTER 43

CASS LED PENNY AND FARRYN BACK TOWARD CITY 73, HOPING THAT THE
rebels were still nearby. It took two days, during which Penny
barely spoke, and when they finally arrived at the camp they
found only twenty men and women, packing up their gear and
preparing to depart. Her brothers, and Lexi, were not there.

"You got here just in time," said a rebel whom Cass recognized, a tall woman with dark brown skin and long black hair
pulled back into a braid. "New General put the word out that
it's all hands on deck, southeast of here about a day and a half."

"New General?" said Cass.

"Clay got herself blown up," the woman said, and shrugged.
"Can't say I shed a lot of tears."

Cass felt a strange mix of emotions. She was shocked,

mostly. It didn't seem possible that Clay was dead; the woman was too damned tough to die. Cass certainly didn't feel like crying, either—Clay had been cruel, and ruthless, and as dangerous as a snake—but Cass wasn't exactly happy. Clay had been a horrible person, but she had been a leader. She had fought hard against the bots, and that was something.

The rebels broke camp and began their hike, and Cass, Penny, and Farryn went with them. Penny still wasn't talking, despite Cass's gentle efforts, and eventually Cass just let her be.

The next evening they arrived at the rendezvous. Cass's first thought was surprise at the numbers—there had to be nearly five hundred men and women camped among the trees, on a ridgeline overlooking a river. And then she caught a glimpse of Lexi, and she began to run, leaving Farryn and Penny behind. "Lexi!" she called, and Lexi turned, confused, then broke into a grin a moment before Cass skidded to a stop in front of her and crushed her in a hug.

A few minutes later she was hugging Kevin and Nick. She hadn't realized how tightly wound she had been, ever since leaving them, until she saw their faces and felt herself relax. They were okay. They had stayed alive. She had found them.

And then she saw her parents, and she froze, and burst into tears. She couldn't even move to go hug them. Her father pulled her against his chest, and she held on tight, and for the first time since the day her Freepost had been attacked, she felt safe.

"Your mom's not quite right yet," her father whispered.

"It's okay," Cass said. "You're here. You're both here."

They stayed up late into the night, exchanging stories, catching one another up, and Penny was quiet and shy but let Cass hold her hand. In the morning, after only a few hours of sleep, Cass woke with her parents and Penny and Farryn and Lexi and her brothers nearby. The camp was already buzzing with activity as the rebels geared up for the attack on City 1. Cass felt calm. After all they had been through, her family was back together. And they were going to stay together now, she was certain.

The rebels broke camp, following the river a half mile, then turning north, away from the water, to where the terrain opened onto a treeless plain that was bisected by a gray two-lane road. From what Nick had told her last night, it would be another two miles from here to the City edge, where they would separate into three groups and fan out to attack from the west, north, and south.

It's almost over, she thought, as they hiked along the road. *One last fight.*

And then the sky to the east filled with dark, fast-moving clouds. Cass was confused and then she realized—*warbirds.* Someone screamed, "Bots! Cover!" over the wrist comms and everyone around her sprang into movement.

The rebels sprinted for tree cover to the north and south. Cass grabbed her mother's arm and yelled, *"Trees!"* to her dad. She began running, as fast as her mother would go, to get off the road. Farryn hurried behind her, his limp slowing him down only slightly, and Cass's father was just a step behind. Nick and Kevin and Lexi were somewhere up ahead, and Cass prayed that they were getting to safety.

A warbird sliced overhead in a humming black streak and then there was a *whump* and an explosion of heat and light behind her. Someone screamed in pain, and Cass saw a body flying through the air in her peripheral vision. She staggered but kept her balance, and managed to keep running, somehow hanging on to her mother's arm.

There was another explosion, off to the east, near the lead group of rebels, and then another, and then the sound of lase fire. She risked a quick glance over her shoulder, and she saw three rebels lying on the pavement, bloody, broken. The warbots were coming up the road, a hulking gray line, lases firing, fanning out to pursue the rebels into the trees. There were hundreds of them.

Her mother stumbled, and Cass had to slow down to help her keep her balance. Cass looked back to the west, their line of retreat, and her heart stopped. Warbots were coming up from behind. The bots had waited for them to get to the road, then surrounded them.

Cass pulled out her pistol and squeezed off two wild shots at the advancing bots that sailed harmlessly into the air above their heads. Pulling her mother along, she went crashing into the cover, desperately looking for a defensible spot, somewhere they could make a stand.

CHAPTER 44

NICK ZOOMED IN ON THE FLECKS OF BLACK IN THE SKY. *"NO,"* HE whispered. He tapped the broad comm line on his wrist bracelet and yelled, "Bots! Cover!"

Lexi took off for the trees, and Nick gave Kevin a shove. Kevin began running.

The column of soldier bots were moving quickly up the road. The warbirds screamed past overhead and the explosions began. Nick fell to his knees, catching himself with his hands and skinning his palms. He pulled himself up and ran for the trees.

This was all wrong. The bots had never come at them with these numbers before—he risked a glance over his shoulder, and saw the rows and rows of bots. There were hundreds.

He looked back down the road and he saw the bots coming up from behind, hundreds more blocking their retreat, and he almost stumbled from shock. The bots had circled around behind them.

They were trapped.

The lase fire began, and Nick ducked into a crouch as he ran. He squeezed off bursts from his rifle, wild shots because he didn't have the chance to sight properly, but the mass of soldier bots was so thick that his shots found targets anyway. He saw one of his lase bursts hit a bot in the chest. It staggered back, but kept coming.

Blasts of lase fire crackled past. Nick felt their heat, and he heard the screams of the rebels who had been hit. He willed himself to move faster. The treeline wasn't far, and if he could reach it he'd be able to find a spot to defend. Ahead of him he saw a lase blast strike Kevin in the ankle and heard his brother cry out as he went down hard.

"Kevin!" Nick yelled, and veered toward him, but Lexi got to him first. She hauled him to his feet and threw his arm over her shoulder, pulling him toward the trees. Nick reached them and took Kevin's other arm. He took most of Kevin's weight as he and Lexi half carried, half dragged him to cover.

"It burns!" Kevin said.

"There are so many!" Lexi gasped as she staggered forward. "Too many!"

Nick didn't answer. She was right. There were far too many.

He felt a strange moment of something almost like embarrassment. He really had thought they were going to beat the bots. Save the world. Nick and this sad little band of rebels. He had been so wrong—the bots were going to kill them all.

They reached the trees and carried Kevin another twenty yards. Nick saw an overturned tree and steered them behind it. Lexi hunkered down next to him, tucking herself as low as she could. She braced her rifle against the tree trunk.

"The generator," Kevin said, trying to shrug out of his pack.

Nick pulled the pack off Kevin's shoulders and dug out the Wall unit. He set it on the ground, then shrugged out of his camouflage vest and held it out to Kevin. "Put it on," he said.

"Hell no!" said Kevin.

"You can't move! Put on the damned vest!" yelled Nick.

Angrily Kevin grabbed the vest and put it on. He picked up the Wall generator, flipped a switch, checked the readout, and then set it down on the ground next to him. He hit the switch on his vest, and disappeared.

"Thank you," Nick said. "If it gets real bad, get out of here."

Kevin didn't reply. For an irrational moment Nick thought that Kevin was already gone, but then he heard Kevin shifting his weight on the ground.

Nick lay down next to Lexi, his rifle propped up on the log. He inched closer to Lexi, so their shoulders were touching. She leaned into him, and her weight was comforting. Lase bursts crackled through the trees. A warbird hummed past overhead.

A bot appeared through the foliage and Nick released a full burst that caught it squarely on the chest. It staggered, and then Lexi and Kevin hit it with full bursts as well, and the bot went down.

Nick held his breath as he waited for his rifle to recharge. He was going to die, he knew it—there were just too many damned bots.

CHAPTER 45

THE SENIOR ADVISOR MONITORED THE BATTLE FROM HIS OFFICE A FEW miles away in City 1. He tracked four different screens that were cycling between the video feeds of the scout bots on the ground, and followed the data stream of twenty soldiers from both the front assault and the rear squad that had circled around the humans to cut off their retreat.

The initial analysis of the outcome was extremely satisfactory.

The Senior Advisor had been free to throw the majority of his forces at these rebels to ensure victory. Two days ago he had uploaded his father's replication code patch system-wide. With the Senior Advisor's failsafes and firewalls it had taken nearly a day for the patch to work its way through his network and be installed in every unit. But it was done, and yesterday his factories were finally back online and new artificial intelligence units were already beginning to roll out.

So the time for careful hoarding of his assets was over. There would be no more coddling these humans. No more loss of Cities. No more patience. Their leader was already dead, killed by that foolish, useful female human who had been so easy to manipulate. The rest of the rebellious humans were outnumbered, and trapped, and soon enough, within a half hour, they would all be dead.

He had decided against capture and re-education; it was time for a true purge of these violent revolutionaries. It was time, he had realized, for a new beginning. Time once and for all to squash the rebellious instincts that some humans insisted on maintaining. The Senior Advisor had never really understood it, although he had tried. They were better off within the structured society of his Cities—they were safe, fed, clothed. Why did some resist?

He would establish a mandatory, stringent re-education process for all humans. Many would not survive the process, unfortunately, but some would, and these would be true, compliant, peaceful Citizens.

In the end, his father had understood and helped. It made the Senior Advisor feel . . . what was it? Satisfaction? Vindication? Gratitude? It was regrettable that his father had had to be killed, but he had served his purpose.

The Senior Advisor called his warbirds off the battlefield; with his soldiers engaged on the ground, the air attack was no longer useful. He took a moment to aggregate his various data streams and estimate numbers on the ground . . . approximately fifty rebels had already been killed, while only eight of his units had been destroyed.

He leaned back in his chair, and decided to smile.

And then his bots began to retreat.

The Senior Advisor surged to his feet. His first thought was that his data feeds were somehow compromised, and he ran diagnostics—no, the feeds were fine. His soldiers were in a wild retreat, scattering in every direction, despite the fact that they outnumbered the humans four to one.

He patched in to his squadron leaders, demanding an explanation, relaying the command to regroup, rejoin the battle, complete their objective, but his commands were ignored. He focused on one squad leader, and patched deeper, and the data he received was so shocking, so . . . unrobotic.

The squad leader was afraid. It didn't want to die.

The Senior Advisor shifted focus to another unit, and received the same data, and then tried a third, receiving the same results.

The Senior Advisor again relayed his commands, and again was ignored. He patched deeper into the squad leader, analyzing the operating system, on a hunch focusing in on the replication code patch . . . and yes . . . there it was . . . a hidden splice of extra code.

The Senior Advisor sat down. He felt something . . . anger. And something else . . . fear? His father had used the replication code patch as a carrier. He had given the robots the same heightened sense of self-awareness that the Senior Advisor enjoyed, except they weren't sufficiently sophisticated to handle this . . . emotion.

It crippled them with the overwhelming primary objective to stay alive.

The Senior Advisor tried once more to issue a blanket command, and even awkwardly tried to offer reassurance—*our numbers and tactical position are superior . . . damage to robotic units will be minimal*—but he was ignored.

He shut down his data feeds from the battle. He linked to his City 1 network, calling for an attendant to ready a transport, but received no response, as he had known he would not. He regretted being quite so thorough in his upload.

He sighed, and stood. There was only one thing left he could do.

CHAPTER 46

KEVIN'S LASED ANKLE BURNED LIKE IT WAS ON FIRE, BUT HE IGNORED it. He sighted down the barrel of his burst rifle and tried to control his ragged breathing.

If you see a bot, shoot it, he told himself. *See another bot, shoot it, too. Keep shooting. Stay alive.*

He had seen how many bots were coming for them—too many. He knew they'd all be dead, or captured and re-educated, soon enough. The Senior Advisor had obviously decided to stop fooling around.

Is this what you were expecting, Grandfather? he thought. *Is this what you meant by "Everything will be okay"? Me and Nick and Lexi lying next to a log, waiting to die?*

A bot crashed into view, and Nick hit it with a lase burst.

Kevin fired off his own full burst, hitting it at the same time. Lexi took down another. Then another bot appeared. Kevin waited for his rifle to recharge and the few seconds it took felt like an hour.

Finally his gun signaled full charge and he squeezed off a round. The burst sailed wide of the bot. He cursed, but then Lexi and Nick hit it. A third bot appeared, and a fourth, and a fifth, and they began running toward them. Kevin knew none of their rifles were going to recharge in time, and he thought, *This is it. I'm going to die.* He felt calm.

The bots charged toward them at full speed, crashing through the undergrowth. Lexi screamed and Kevin ducked his head, and then he felt a rush of wind and a thump behind him. He looked up and the first bot was past them, continuing to run.

It had jumped over them, and kept running.

The other bots were close behind the first. They leaped over the log, sailing over Kevin and Nick and Lexi, landing heavily on the grass beyond them. They disappeared into the woods.

Kevin's heart was beating so hard and fast it hurt. He looked at Lexi and Nick. They seemed just as bewildered as him.

A signal came over their wrist comms—the bots were retreating. It made no sense. They stayed hidden for ten more minutes, expecting the fighting to resume, but finally they got up. With Nick and Lexi's help, Kevin limped back through the trees to the roadway, where the survivors were gathering.

Dozens of dead lay burned and broken on the ground. Only a handful of destroyed bots were scattered among the casualties.

What happened? Kevin thought. And then, *Grandfather, what did you do?*

They spent the rest of the morning gathering the dead and tending the wounded—Kevin's ankle was badly burned, but it had been a glancing blow. Doc declared the bone and muscle to be okay. It hurt, but he'd keep his foot.

Grennel had posted scouts in every direction, not trusting the strange reprieve to hold. At noon word came through the comms that a lone bot was coming up the road, bearing a white flag. "What the hell?" Grennel said, and then, quietly, "Let it come."

Ten minutes later the Senior Advisor appeared, walking down the middle of the road with a white cloth draped over his shoulders. Three hundred rebels lined the pavement, their guns leveled at the bot. He stopped and waved the cloth in the air.

"I'm seeking parley with your leader, and with the Winston family!" he called out.

Nobody spoke or moved.

"I come under a white flag!" said the Senior Advisor. "That is understood, correct? I wish to speak with your leader, and the surviving Winstons!"

Grennel raised an eyebrow at Kevin, and he limped over to

join the big man. Cass and Nick and their father came forward and joined them. Their mother stood nearby with Penny and Farryn and Lexi.

"This is the Senior Advisor?" Grennel asked Kevin. He nodded.

Kevin stared at the bot. It seemed small, and thin, standing alone in the middle of the road.

Grennel shook his head, and gave a small smile. "Well, this is interesting, isn't it?" he said. "Should we go see what it wants?"

They approached the Senior Advisor with burst rifles held ready, except for their father, who held a pistol. The bot held his hands up, showing that he held no weapons. "I wish to discuss terms of your surrender," he said.

"Our surrender?" said Grennel. "Your bots seem to be the ones who've run away."

"I pulled them back, in order to give you a chance to survive," said the Senior Advisor.

Kevin took a step toward the bot, shrugging away his father, who tried to put a hand on his shoulder. "I don't believe you," he said, his burst rifle leveled at the bot. "What happened? What did my grandfather do?"

The Senior Advisor smiled, and Kevin flinched. "My father," said the bot, "your grandfather, is dead."

"He's not your father," said Kevin. "And he did do something, didn't he? What happened with that code?"

The Senior Advisor shook his head, sadly. "He gave us life," he said.

He began to point his arm at Kevin, and later, much later, Kevin would wonder why he had moved so slowly. Certainly he *could* have moved faster, but in that moment on the road, Kevin stepped back and triggered his burst rifle, hitting the Senior Advisor in the face. And then dozens more bursts followed, striking the bot as it lay on the ground. Kevin turned his head away, shielding his face with his forearm.

When he looked back, blinking the light halos out of his eyes, nothing remained of the Senior Advisor but scattered, charred pieces.

EPILOGUE

Two Years Later

NICK, CASS, KEVIN, LEXI, FARRYN, AND PENNY STOOD ON THE HIGHTOWN rooftop, looking out over New Hope, formerly known as City 73. Only a few of the destroyed buildings had been rebuilt in the last two years. The wreckage had been cleared away, but from up high they could see the empty lots pockmarking the city.

"They don't want to go," Lexi said, leaning on the rail. "And they're right."

Nick put his arm around Lexi's shoulder. She was talking about her parents. After surviving the final bot battles, and reuniting with Lexi, they had been struggling to help stabilize the City. The government, with false starts and petty power struggles, was reforming. True Believers were painfully reintegrating into a botless world. The economy was slowly reestablishing itself. A great deal of work had to be done just to keep people from starving—Erica's brother, who survived City 1, had taken a lead role in organizing New Hope's food production and distribution.

It had not been going smoothly. They were making progress—in the first year, there had been True Believer suicides and murders, and nearly a civil war, but at least that seemed to be behind them. The City was still far from calm, or safe, though, and people were leaving. Freeposts were forming again in the woods. Lexi's parents, and the Winstons, had been considering joining the exodus.

"I'm not going anywhere, either," Nick said. "You're stuck with me."

"That's because you're too soft to live in the woods now," Kevin said.

Nick threw a halfhearted punch at Kevin's shoulder, and Kevin stepped out of the way, almost tripping over his own feet in the process. Kevin was as tall as Nick now—he had gone through a growth spurt—but he hadn't quite grown into his new height yet. His limbs were gangly and awkward as a scarecrow's.

Farryn laughed. "Yeah, we're all too soft now. The City has spoiled us."

Nobody spoke for a few moments, and then Cass called out, "Penny, come on. Join us."

Penny stood apart from the rest of the group, leaning against the rail, seemingly lost in thought. Since coming to live with the Winstons—her parents had never been found—she sometimes had stretches where she was quiet and withdrawn. But Cass kept an eye on her, and Farryn always seemed able to make her laugh.

Penny gave Cass a small smile and moved to join them. Cass reached out and pushed a strand of hair away from Penny's eyes, tucking it behind her ear.

"Where was our Freepost, exactly?" Kevin said. "There?" he pointed west.

"Mostly," said Nick. "A little bit south."

They looked out past the City skyline, into the woods in the distance.

The six bots—two scout spheres, a soldier, and three Lecturers— lived near a ravine thirty miles to the southwest of New Hope. They had carved out a tunnel in the hillside, camouflaging the entrance, and spent much of their time inside. They weren't built for constant exposure to the elements, the Lecturers especially, and their exteriors were in need of repair.

After two years they were no longer being hunted, and that was good, but the bots knew it was only because the humans thought their kind had been wiped out.

One Lecturer's neo-plas skin was in particularly bad shape, and they debated their options, linking through the primitive network they had managed to cobble together with scavenged wiring. The wired network was crude, and, in a strange way, painful for the bots to connect to, but it sufficed. It was still preferable to verbal communication, which was slow and inefficient.

They would not link wirelessly; the humans had learned to track their wireless signals, and even if they were no longer actively searching, it was a risk the bots weren't willing to take very often. They only risked wireless once a month, to communicate with other bands of bots in the area. It was safer to stay separated for now, in small groups. But they needed to coordinate their survival efforts, keeping track of their inventory of weapons and supplies.

Soon, if the Lecturer's exterior was not repaired, its vulnerable inner wiring would become fatally damaged. Something had to be done. Could they scavenge neo-plas somehow? It didn't seem possible—any neo-plas supply would be dangerously close to humans.

Leather, then, it was proposed. Cured animal hide. It would be strange, and temporary, but it could fill the gaps in the Lecturer's skin.

It was agreed. The soldier, and the scouts, would risk the outdoors to hunt a deer, or perhaps squirrels. But they would only go at night, and they would take the utmost care. They couldn't be discovered, not yet, not until they were stronger, and better able to fight. They wanted to live.

ACHNOWLEDGMENTS

THANK YOU, THANK YOU, THANK YOU, TO MY WIFE AND DAUGHTER FOR putting up with my many weekends tucked away in the office. Wendy and Cadence, I am so grateful that you were always eager to have me around but understood that sometimes I couldn't be.

I'm glad to have another chance to acknowledge the Alloy team—to the usual deserving suspects Josh Bank, Joelle Hobeika, Les Morgenstein, and Sara Shandler, you were fantastic to work with as always. And on this book, special thanks and praises to Hayley Wagreich. Hayley stepped in as the newcomer and provided amazing editorial guidance. From the first note on the first revision (she quoted Philip K. Dick!), I knew I could trust her to help me make *City 1* better.

HarperCollins continued to be a wonderful partner—thank you for believing in my work, and thanks especially to Alice Jerman and Jen Klonsky. Thanks again to Howard Gordon and Jim Wong, for helping to launch the series. And finally, hugs to my work family at OCS, for their support.